"WHAT DO YOU WANT FROM ME, ALI?"

"I want the truth about yourself, Nolan. I want to know who you are and what kind of danger you're in. Is that too much to ask?"

"The more you know, the more you'll be involved. I can't take that chance."

"You think I'm not already involved? I'm in love with you."

The corner of his mouth twitched in sharp reaction to her declaration. They had never talked of love, only of caring and needing—and desire.

"Go back to Tulsa in the morning and forget about me," he muttered.

Her eyes were full of pain. "Can you walk away and forget your feelings for me?"

"Given time, yes. I'll forget about you, Ali."

"I don't believe that!" she cried. "And I don't think you do, either."

CANDLELIGHT ECSTASY CLASSIC ROMANCES

CANDLELIGHT ECSTASY ROMANCES®

BITTERSWEET TORMENT

Vanessa Richards

Copyright © ... [illegible] ... All rights reserved. No part of this book may be reproduced or transmitted in any form or by any means, electronic or mechanical, including photocopying, recording, or by any information storage and retrieval system, without the written permission of the Publisher, except where permitted by law.

Dell ® TM 681510, Dell Publishing Co., Inc.

Candlelight Ecstasy Romance ®, 1,203,540, is a registered trademark of Dell Publishing Co., Inc., New York, New York.

ISBN: 0-440-10820-9

Printed in the United States of America

February 1983

10 9 8 7 6 5 4 3 2 1

WFH

A CANDLELIGHT ECSTASY ROMANCE®

Published by
Dell Publishing Co., Inc.
1 Dag Hammarskjold Plaza
New York, New York 10017

Dell ® TM 681510, Dell Publishing Co., Inc.

Candlelight Ecstasy Romance®, 1,203,540, is a registered
trademark of Dell Publishing Co., Inc., New York, New York.

ISBN: 0-440-10820-9

Printed in the United States of America

February 1987

10 9 8 7 6 5 4 3 2 1

WFH

*To Larry, for encouraging me in the
beginning
and
For Ty and Tara, to show that they can
accomplish anything with both patience and
perseverance
and
To Mom and Dad for some way, unknown to
me, instilling that same quality in their
daughter.*

To Our Readers:

We have been delighted with your enthusiastic response to Candlelight Ecstasy Romances®, and we thank you for the interest you have shown in this exciting series.

In the upcoming months we will continue to present the distinctive sensuous love stories you have come to expect only from Ecstasy. We look forward to bringing you many more books from your favorite authors and also the very finest work from new authors of contemporary romantic fiction.

As always, we are striving to present the unique, absorbing love stories that you enjoy most—books that are more than ordinary romance. Your suggestions and comments are always welcome. Please write to us at the address below.

Sincerely,

The Editors
Candlelight Romances
1 Dag Hammarskjold Plaza
New York, New York 10017

CHAPTER ONE

Five stories up, her silhouette framed by the window-pane, Alinda Sterling observed the toylike figures on the street below. They were testimonials that life continued, no matter how hard she wished for it to stand still. No, not to stand still. She wanted the clock turned back. She wanted to stop waking up in the middle of the night to call Jackson's name only to have her heart sink with disappointment as the stark reality crept into her half-wakefulness.

The afternoon sun haloed around her as she stood analyzing her attitude. For a woman who had always had her way, this was a bitter pill to swallow. She wasn't feeling sorry for herself. It was more a feeling of being cheated. Yes, that was it. Cheated.

She had moved from grief to anger and she wondered if the resigned acceptance that the hospital chaplain had spoken of would ever come. Admittedly, her being here was a small step toward acceptance.

The hand that came to rest on her shoulder was an

9

intrusion, although she knew it was meant to comfort. There was nothing very striking about the man that had been Jackson's friend since high school. The brown hair and small physique didn't cause heads to turn when he entered the courtroom, unless you knew him. He had been her rock and she mustered a faint smile for him.

"I'm glad you decided to get this out of the way." Her lawyer, Robert Cameron, broke the silence he had endured for the past five minutes. "It's been two months since Jackson passed away. That's too long to stay cooped up in the house."

"It's called mourning."

Robert turned her to face him, a firm grip on her shoulders as their eyes met at the same level. "You had seven wonderful years with your husband. Be grateful for that, Alinda. Some couples never have even one."

"And we had fourteen miserable months with Jackson in constant pain, in and out of the hospital, and finally the last month in a coma," she countered, her bitterness surfacing. "Some couples never have that either!"

The roaring in her ears intensified. She was so tired. She turned back to the window and tried to control her bitterness, but her nerves were frayed and she was in no mood to be reasonable. Not even with the man that had stood by her when her whole world was crumbling around her.

A roughly handsome man unfolded his length from his truck on the street below. His cowboy boots were spit-polished to a high sheen. Alinda watched as he took note of his surroundings—the older couple at the bus stop, the man using the pay phone at the curb to the south, and the young pregnant woman leaving the office building. When he reached the entrance, he paused and took one last surreptitious look over his shoulder.

There was a stirring of recognition in the back of Alinda's mind. She chewed at the berry-red color on her lips as she struggled to place the thick blond hair and weathered features of the man who ducked through the doors of Cameron, Cameron & Phyfe.

Glancing at her watch, her irritation at being kept waiting grew. Taking advantage of Robert's friendship and pleading complete exhaustion, Alinda had put off discussing Jackson's estate for two months. If not for Robert's urging, she would have put it off forever. But he was right. There were decisions to be made and now that she was here, she wanted to get it over with. Turning to her lawyer, she let some of her irritation show, "Exactly who is it we're waiting for, Robert?"

"He's only ten minutes late, Alinda. Relax. Come and sit down." He motioned to one of the matching chairs in front of his modern desk. "Would you like some tea?"

"I'd rather have a cigarette." She was weary to the bone, but too restless to sit down. She helped herself to the gold case on Robert's desk, ignoring his disapproving look as he leaned across the desk to light it for her. Alinda's hands shook imperceptibly as she brought the cigarette to her lips and inhaled deeply. It made her realize this meeting was stirring up a lot of feelings she had thought she had come to terms with weeks ago.

Unannounced, a man entered. "Mr. Cameron." He extended his right hand. "Sorry I'm late. There was a pileup on the bypass." He ran his fingers through his hair, bringing little order to the unruly waves too long for today's style. "Traffic was backed up for miles."

Alinda recognized him as the man she had seen from the window and knew why he had looked familiar. Her puzzled expression was not for *who* he was, but for *why*

11

the foreman of their ranch was here for the reading of Jackson's will.

"Mr. Taylor, I believe you've met Mrs. Sterling."

Nolan faced Alinda and nodded. He stood several inches taller than her five feet eight inches. He was the picture of earthy strength and virility, his skin tanned a smooth bronze from many hours spent outdoors, making Alinda feel pale in comparison.

With experienced eyes, Nolan searched for what was hidden behind the artificial color of skillfully applied makeup. He felt sure he would discover natural beauty similar to that found in a finely carved cameo. He had an unusual desire to see if his instincts were correct. Her alabaster skin lent her a certain vulnerability, yet her jet black hair and obsidian eyes were striking to distraction. "I wish we were meeting again under different circumstances. Jackson was a good man and a good friend." Nolan extended both his hands and clasped hers. She was like a fine china doll and he felt strangely awkward.

Alinda's raven eyebrow arched suspiciously. She had only heard her husband mention Nolan Taylor's name a few times and it was always related to ranch business, never anything personal, and yet, Mr. Taylor had emphasized the word *friend*. Was he serious or just being polite?

Robert motioned to the chairs opposite his desk. "I know the reading of the will is not a pleasant task. I'm sure you both would like to put it behind you." The lawyer moved to his chair with an air of propriety and settled a pair of wire-rimmed glasses on his nose. He recited the legal document as if by heart. It was twenty minutes before Alinda discovered the reason for Nolan Taylor's presence at the reading of her husband's will.

"To sum it up, Jackson leaves everything to you, Alinda, except the ranch, which he leaves to Mr. Taylor." Robert pinned Alinda with his eyes after pushing his glasses back to the bridge of his nose.

"You mean Indian Paintbrush?" Alinda asked bewilderedly. At the lawyer's nod, she said, "That doesn't make sense, Robert." Her mouth went slack as she silently questioned the lawyer and then her accusing eyes bored into Nolan. "Did you know about this?"

"I'm as surprised as you are," Nolan answered quietly.

Alinda made a disbelieving noise in her throat. Why would Jackson do this? Was there more to his and Mr. Taylor's relationship than she knew? And even if there was, why didn't Jackson tell her his plans? It wasn't like him. They had always shared everything. Or had they? It hurt to think there might have been other things that he had deliberately kept from her. No! She would not believe he was deceitful. Not without a very good reason.

"How long did you know my husband?"

Nolan's calm blue eyes met Alinda's turbulent rounded ones. "Not quite two years." He had covertly studied the woman next to him during the reading of the will. His fingers had itched to remove the decorative combs that held her coal-black hair away from her face. It was a face too thin for perfection, but not for elegance. There were soft hollows beneath her cheeks that made him want, beyond all reasoning, to run a finger along the shaded crevice. Her legs crossed at the knees, drawing his attention downward to where her dress had ridden up her nylon-clad thigh. This is madness, he thought, and forced his mind back to the problem at hand when Alinda demanded, "Where from?"

This inheritance was an unexpected turn of events and he could tell by Mrs. Sterling's expression that she was going to be trouble. He read the hostility and mistrust in her eyes and he had to smile to himself. *If she only knew*

13

the truth about me, her suspicions would be laughable. It was an amusing thought until the gravity of the situation sank in, then he cursed silently. Every time he was settled in, something happened to call attention to him and he had the feeling this time wasn't going to be an exception. His mouth hardened as he sat straighter in the modern barrel chair and finally answered belligerently, "It's irrelevant where we met."

"I think it is relevant." Angered all the more by his evasiveness, Alinda confronted Robert. "We're talking about a six-figure operation. My husband wouldn't give it away to a man he barely knows." She searched Robert's face for agreement, but all she found was his courtroom-defense expression, totally unreadable. "For God's sake, Robert. You've known him all your life. He was never prone to whims." Defensive herself, Alinda stood and clutched the edge of the desk, her head swimming with the sudden movement. "At least never . . . never before he became ill." She turned away from the two men, blinking back the tears that glistened in her dark eyes, and feeling completely alone.

She wasn't going to let this stranger walk off with Indian Paintbrush and make a fool of Jackson, not without a fight. She pictured the gently rolling hills of the ranch, covered with the wildflowers it was named for and the whitewashed home flanked with honeysuckle and fronted by a long wooden porch. No. Not without a fight, she vowed.

It was not the ranch itself, although losing it did tug at her heart. Financially it meant nothing to her. What made her fighting mad was the thought of a man—a virtual stranger to her—actually benefiting from Jackson's very painful misfortune. She hated to think that he wasn't completely rational during the last months of his life, but it was true. "When did Jackson make this change in his will? Before or after he found out about his illness?"

"Three months before he went into the hospital for the last time." Robert shifted in his chair and leaned forward. "But you must understand, Alinda, we made several changes. Jackson's will hadn't been updated in over two years. Naturally, when he found out he might only have six months to a year to live, he wanted everything in order."

Still directing her questions to the lawyer, she asked, "Was Mr. Taylor mentioned in the will before that?"

Alinda was deliberately ignoring Nolan and he was content to sit back and watch the exchange in silence. It was obvious that the strain was getting to the woman who stood proud and angry beside him. He hadn't decided whether her anger was prompted by greed or out of true love and loyalty for her dead husband. In his profession, he had had to be an expert at reading people and analyzing their motives. He studied the look of confusion and sorrow in Alinda's huge doe eyes and decided if she was acting, she was good, real good.

Rising to face her, he became even more aware of her frailty. She reminded him of a swan, sleek and graceful, her bearing almost regal despite her loss of composure. He waited for her response when Robert answered her question with a negative shake of his head.

"And just like that"—she snapped her tapered fingers in mid-air—"he left him a hundred acres of prime grazing land, not to mention three producing gas wells, and several hundred head of cattle?" She laughed humorlessly and faced Nolan with disdain. "I find it very hard to believe that you didn't take advantage of his illness to persuade him to do this."

Nolan's temper flared for the first time. "No one could have taken advantage of Jackson Sterling, and if you don't know that, you're not the wife he described to me."

Alinda blanched at his accusation. She couldn't imagine Jackson discussing her with the foreman of their ranch. *But to a good friend?* Mr. Taylor was partially right, she conceded. Jackson was too shrewd to be taken advantage of by an amateur. But is Nolan Taylor an amateur? There were too many pieces missing. One fact remained: Jackson had not confided in her and the only reason would be to protect her. *From what?* Her mind screamed in frustration.

"I'm going to contest the will, Robert." She saw the lawyer's eyes narrow and held her hand up to stop his forthcoming interruption. "I know you're thinking that I've inherited twenty times what this ranch is worth. Why can't I be content? Well, I'll tell you." She turned to Nolan and pointed. "I won't let a—a *stranger* steal Indian Paintbrush right out from under Jackson." She was shaking, her voice high-pitched with the tremendous emotional buildup. "He was so heavily sedated most of those months he hardly knew who he was at times." Her eyes pleaded with Robert for understanding. "You know it's true!"

"I wouldn't have let him change his will if I didn't think he was completely rational, Alinda." Her friend's voice was unflinching. For a small man, he could command a person's attention with his eyes alone. Alinda felt the full force of his censure, but still would not back down.

"Why don't we sleep on this before we take any further steps?" Robert suggested.

"Yes, it's been a surprise to both of us." Their eyes met and Nolan's heart tightened in his chest. Underneath her

16

tough, aristocratic bearing, she was a delicate woman, barely hanging on, using anger as a shield against what fate had dealt her. For a moment, he found himself feeling sorry for her. "After we've had some time to think about this, maybe we can find a compromise."

"Don't patronize me, Mr. Taylor. If you think you're getting away with this, you can just think again!" Their condescension only added fuel to her anger.

"I think Mrs. Sterling and I should discuss this in private and I'll get back to you later in the week." Robert rose in a dismissing gesture.

Nolan nodded and shook Robert's extended hand. "I'm sure we can come to an agreement." He stressed his position as much for the lawyer's sake as Mrs. Sterling's. There was no way he could afford the notoriety a lawsuit would bring. He would sign it all over to her before she reached the point of suing him.

The bright sun momentarily blinded him as he exited the dimly lit building. He cursed and quickly blinked, forcing his eyes to adjust to the afternoon light.

This past year he had let down his guard, having kept a low profile and feeling relatively secure living at the isolated ranch. But, he thought, some old habits were hard to break, as, with an eye for detail, he searched the parking area and the streets for anything or anyone suspicious.

Finding nothing unusual about his surroundings, he left the protection of the building behind him and headed for his truck. He paused in his motion of starting the nondescript vehicle to observe the woman leaving the office building.

There was no fire, yet his whole body felt aflame as he watched Jackson's widow cross the parking lot to a cream-colored Mercedes. He stirred uncomfortably in his

17

seat. He knew what it was to be hungry for a woman, but he had never experienced this burning desire for something he couldn't even name.

Suddenly, he wondered if he had missed out on something in his forty-one years by not knowing a woman's love and devotion as Jackson had. He shook off the feeling and turned the key in the ignition. No woman had ever made him pause long enough to ask himself that question and he didn't like the fact that a prominent widow had lit a fire in him. There was no place for a woman in his life. The past four years had proven that.

Alinda followed the circular drive and parked in front of her Tudor-style home that was almost hidden from the street by stately oak and pecan trees.

As she walked up the steps she thought about Robert's suggestions regarding Jackson's will. He wanted her to let it stand, uncontested, regaling her of the outcome of similar cases and the adverse publicity a court battle was sure to bring. Even so, the whole scenario still nagged at her, creating the feeling that there was more to this than a sick man's last-minute generosity.

One foot paused at the top step. She was tired. In the past year, she had fought with doctors and nurses, Jackson's business associates, and even Robert. She had been forced to make decisions she wanted Jackson to get well enough to make for himself. She wasn't sure she had the strength left to fight Nolan Taylor too.

The heavy wooden door clicked shut behind her. The tapping of her heels echoed as she crossed the marble-tiled entry and started up the winding staircase.

"Mrs. Sterling, I didn't hear you drive up."

"Hello, Mary. Is Marguerite still here?"

"Yes. This is her late day."

18

"Will you tell her I want a tuna salad sandwich and a glass of ice water?" Alinda paused halfway up the stairs. She would need all her strength if she planned to take on Nolan Taylor. Something warned her he would be a tough adversary. "Mary, make that a roast beef, some cheese and fruit on the side and a large glass of milk."

Mary Hensley, the Sterlings' housekeeper for the past six years, hid her surprise. "Yes, ma'am."

Alinda's bedroom created a welcoming atmosphere with salmon-colored carpet, peach-washed walls and azure blue and cream accents throughout. In the dressing area, she slipped out of her burgundy cashmere suit and matching silk blouse. The equally expensive satin lingerie followed.

She glimpsed at the reflection of her figure in the mirror-covered closet doors and lingered to critically assess the changes. She hadn't noticed how thin she had become. There was no longer a rounded fullness in her breasts; her hips and legs had a coltish-thin look rather than a shapely feminine one. At the tap on the door, she grabbed her caftan and called out, "Come in."

Her resolve to eat wavered at the sight of the mound of beef between two thick slices of a kaiser roll. "Did you fix this, Mary?" Alinda's teasing smile was filled with warmth for the housekeeper. "I didn't want the whole roast."

"You need fattening up. A stiff Oklahoma wind would blow you away." Mary set the sterling tray laden with crystal on a small round table. "I bet you've lost ten pounds and that's ten more than you could afford."

Alinda stabbed a fresh pineapple chunk and brought it to her mouth. "You're right. I do look positively awful."

The housekeeper nodded as if her employer had finally come to her senses before quietly leaving Alinda to puzzle out the relationship between Jackson and Nolan Taylor. What reasoning had Nolan used to persuade her husband to leave the foreman Indian Paintbrush? And if she found out, what could she do about it?

Half of the sandwich was eaten before she abandoned her meal and moved purposefully toward the telephone. "Robert, this is Alinda Sterling. I'm glad I caught you." Anxious to get to the point, she continued, "I want you to see what you can find out about this Nolan Taylor."

"I thought we agreed to sleep on it."

"Humor me, Robert. My instincts tell me there's more to him than meets the eye." She changed the receiver to her other ear, then added, "I'm going to find out the truth with or without your help."

"If he's clean, will you drop this and get on with your life?"

Alinda was quiet for a moment. Getting on with her life was a frightening prospect. It stretched in front of her endless and empty.

"Are you going to hire an investigator?" she asked testily.

"You know I am." He sighed.

"Thank you." There was another lull in the conversation, neither knowing how to end it after the awkwardness. "You'll call me as soon as you know something?"

"I don't know what you think you're going to find, but yes, I'll call."

"Good." Alinda replaced the receiver thoughtfully. Was she doing this because she hated the thought of losing Indian Paintbrush? No. The ranch had never meant as much to her as it had to Jackson, but still, she couldn't let a perfect stranger take it without first making sure Jackson had left it to Nolan Taylor of his own free will.

As the days passed, all of her energy was channeled into one purpose—working out the Sterling-Taylor mystery. She had an insatiable curiosity. At times she was even able to laugh at the outrageous conclusions she drew. But there were also times when she grew pensive about the serious repercussions if she decided that Jackson had indeed been conned by Nolan Taylor.

One day meshed with the next. Alinda became more and more impatient waiting for the investigator's report. She decided she had to resume her routine. Her sandals whispered across the slate floor of her sun porch as she passed the matching wicker sofas with bright cushions and an odd assortment of terra-cotta urns decoratively displayed at one end. She stooped over to inhale the musky scent of a large potted geranium that bubbled over its container beneath the windowsill before she sat down behind her wicker desk and flipped the last day of May over to reveal June's hectic pace.

There was the preview of Halston's summer collection, a gallery opening, a cocktail party, and numerous other engagements. She wouldn't make an appearance at any of the functions she had penciled in the date book. Her desire to socialize had dwindled down to nothing. If the truth were known, she had always done it for Jackson. The endless whirl of social obligations was not something that she enjoyed.

She picked up the picture on the corner of her desk. It was taken on their last cruise. Alinda was laughing, her head tilted, her eyes riveted on Jackson's. There were no tears this time as she examined it, only wonderfully fond memories that brought a sad smile to her face.

Suddenly restless, she replaced the picture and crossed to the glass doors that looked out over the pool and grounds, bathed in the freshness of the summer sun. The wind was blowing tiny ripples across the pool's surface.

A light rap on the door interrupted her ideas for a quiet vacation. It was just as well, she told herself, because when it came right down to it, she wouldn't go anyway.

"Alinda, are you in here?" The dark-headed woman peeked into the sunny room. "Oh, there you are."

Turning away from the window, Alinda's sandals slapped against her heels as she advanced toward her sister. "Hi, Jan. I didn't hear the chimes."

"I slipped in the back and told Mary I would find you myself." Jan was a shorter, older version of her sister. They shared the same dark eyes and hair, the same prominent cheekbones, but that was where the resemblance stopped. Jan was effervescent, bubbly, and outgoing; Alinda was quiet, thoughtful, and imaginative.

"How are you?" Alinda asked as they settled into overstuffed chintz cushions.

"Fine."

"Are the kids looking forward to summer vacation?"

"Yes. I came to see how you are, so don't try to sidetrack me with talk of the kids."

"As you can see, I'm fine."

"You do look as if you've put on a few pounds. Why are you still keeping yourself locked away in this house?"

"I've had a lot of things to take care of."

"Like what?" Jan persisted.

When Alinda was not quick enough with her answer, Jan said, "That's what I thought."

Alinda was annoyed with herself for not thinking quicker. She didn't want Jan worrying about her and the last thing she wanted was another lecture.

"I need your help."

22

"With what?"

"We're having a big bash at the country club. They put me in charge and you know what a blank I draw when it comes to creative thinking. That was always your forte."

"I'm sure you can find plenty of willing volunteers."

"None as talented as you."

"No." The needlepoint pillow Alinda had hugged to her was tossed aside and she rose impatiently.

"It's an emergency fund raiser for the Children's Hospital," Jan coaxed, undaunted by her sister's initial refusal. "Just say you'll think about it."

The younger sister hesitated. It was for a good cause. "All right. I'll think about it, but I'm not committing myself, yet."

"Sure, honey," Jan said smugly. "Let's have lunch on Monday and discuss it." She stood and clutched her leather bag under her arm. "Seriously, Alinda, you've got to start getting involved again."

"I am involved." Alinda ushered Jan to the door. "Don't get up on your soapbox or you'll make me late for my story time at the hospital."

She rushed upstairs to change, thinking of the many satisfying hours over the past five years she had spent reading to the children at the hospital. She hadn't been there since Jackson's death, almost three months ago. Jan was right, it was time she started making plans for the future.

Over the next two weeks, reading to the children became a part of her regular routine. The little girls filled an empty space in her heart with hopeful smiles and the boys' bashfulness never failed to lighten her mood. They were eager for attention and she had it to give—in abundance.

She entered the house late one afternoon to find her

mail and phone messages stacked neatly on her desk. She flipped through the messages quickly, pausing to pluck out Robert's before shuffling through the rest and dropping them on the desk top. She eyed the Swiss clock on the opposite wall and dialed his home number. The voice that answered sounded tired. "Robert, this is Alinda. I'm sorry to disturb you at home. Have you found out something on Nolan Taylor?" For days, Alinda had put the subject on the back burner, but she had not forgotten about it.

"So far the information is sketchy."

Alinda adjusted the phone in the crook of her shoulder and stooped to extract a pencil and paper from the drawer. "Tell me what you have."

"He apparently moved here from Colorado twenty-one months ago and immediately went to work as foreman at Indian Paintbrush."

"You've had an investigator working on this case for a month and that's all he reported?" Alinda dropped the pencil on top of the pad.

"It's as if the man only appeared on earth a few days before he arrived at the ranch."

"Robert, he's at least forty years old. There's got to be more."

"I'm supposed to hear from Dave Hailey again on Monday. He's a top-notch detective. I've used him on other cases. I'm sure he'll come up with more information."

"I'll expect a call on Monday then. Have a nice weekend."

After echoing Robert's good-bye, Alinda depressed the button attached to the receiver, disconnecting them. *How could there be no background information on the man?*

Within a few seconds, she had decided to do a little snooping of her own.

She quickly looked up the number she needed. Upon hearing the dial tone, she punched out the appropriate digits.

It rang as she tapped out a beat with the pencil against the desk's edge in an anxious rhythm. *Could he be using an alias? And if he is, why?* All the possibilities were churning in her head and she was caught off guard when the husky baritone finally said, "Yes?"

The nervous action of the pencil was suddenly stilled, but the pace of her heartbeat picked up the tempo. "Mr. Taylor?"

CHAPTER TWO

Alinda stepped from the shower and briskly toweled herself dry. It had been one month since she had made a conscious effort to eat a balanced diet and was rewarded with four pounds when she stepped on the scales.

She slipped into a sleek teddy and covered it with a white eyelet blouse and white linen slacks. They made a startling contrast to her raven hair, equally dark eyes, and olive skin.

The housekeeper's humming drifted to Alinda and she followed the off-key melody to the kitchen. "Good morning," she greeted as she entered the sky-lit room with its ferns and hanging copper pans.

Alinda sat down to the cheese omelet Mary had prepared for breakfast. "I'm going to Indian Paintbrush today. Why don't you take a few days off?"

"Do you think that's wise, going to the ranch I mean?" Mary asked.

"I can't just sit back and do nothing." Contemplatively, she ate her eggs, wishing she had never confided in her housekeeper about Jackson's will and how it all mystified her. "I don't think woman's intuition is admissible court evidence."

The older woman shook her head. "I'll go with you then."

Smiling at Mary's thoughtfulness, Alinda said, "No. You haven't had any free time lately." Alinda sipped her juice and studied the housekeeper who had become her friend in the past six months. Mary had always waited up for Alinda no matter how late she had arrived home from the hospital, ready to listen or just sit quietly by her side, sharing a cup of tea.

"Why are you fixing breakfast? Where is Marguerite?"

"Her little boy is sick. She should be back tomorrow."

"Tell her she can take the whole weekend off. I shouldn't be home until Monday morning." She dabbed at her lips with a linen napkin. "Tell Jasper to bring my car around front, please. I'll get my bag." She pushed away from the table and paused at the door. "Lock up the house and let everyone go for a long weekend, Mary."

"I will. Have a safe trip."

Her bag stowed in the trunk, Alinda steered the luxury car onto the busy street. The city's traffic lights were soon behind her and the Muskogee Turnpike stretched for miles ahead. It was nearly a two-hour drive so Alinda set the cruise control and let her right foot rest comfortably on the floorboard.

Yesterday, Nolan Taylor's voice had been full of vitality over the phone. She wondered if it was the fresh country air or nervous anticipation of their eventual confrontation.

She had simply told him of her desire to remove a few personal things from the main ranch house and he had given her an open invitation, even going as far as to say

27

she could come and go as she pleased and inviting her to stay the night. He was a puzzling man. Was his amiable attitude supposed to throw her off?

She located the exit road to the ranch and turned south. She had not mentioned her intentions concerning the ranch. She hoped to lull him into a false sense of security, thereby getting him to reveal the mystery he was cloaked in. It never occurred to Alinda to be afraid of Nolan Taylor. It was his greed that was suspect, not his sanity.

The sprawling ranch house evoked a lot of memories Alinda had not prepared herself for and she slowed the car in front, fighting the emotions that washed over her.

After trying the front and back doors with no luck, she let the screen door slam to its frame and followed the overgrown path that forked away from the main house.

The morning air was crisp and the walk exhilarating. The dark jade of pines and wild cedar dotted the rolling meadows that undulated for miles around.

She filled her lungs with the pine-scented air, but she could not keep the tension from building with each step she took. A few minutes later, after skirting the barn and several corrals, the path ended at Nolan Taylor's back porch.

She knocked and waited several nerve-wracking seconds before trying the knob. It wasn't locked. Peeking around the open door, she called out his name. No answer. Her heart pounded in her chest as she stepped over a pile of laundry in the kitchen and called anxiously, "Mr. Taylor?" She knew subconsciously she had purposely forgotten her key, hoping for this very opportunity.

There was a coffee pot on the stove and nothing but a toaster and a radio on the counter. A drop-leaf table was in front of the window overlooking the barns and corrals. She ventured into the living area and found two overstuffed chairs facing a small television and divided by a footstool with a few magazines on top. An old desk with the contents hidden by its rolltop was pushed against one blank wall. Nothing adorned the lone cedar beam above the stone fireplace. The only thing that gave the room any life at all was the rainbow-colored book covers in the shelves flanking the fireplace. If he had read all these books, he had spent many hours reading, she thought. His taste was eclectic. Nothing led her any closer to the background of Nolan Taylor. She reached to take a spy novel from the shelf.

"What are you doing in here?"

She jumped guiltily and mumbled an apology as her hand dropped to her side. "I . . ." she searched for the reason that she had come, but the piercing look in his hard blue eyes drove everything from her mind.

"If you're here to discuss the disposition of the ranch, or to clear out some of your things, that's fine. But if you're here to pry into something that's none of your business, you can leave right now!"

Alinda stiffened as if she had been slapped. She was accustomed to a tone altogether different from the stern, censorial one that Nolan used. "I wasn't prying," she protested indignantly.

There was an angry gleam in his eyes that was impossible to misconstrue, but he let her denial stand while he lit the flame under the aluminum pot on the stove and took two cups from the cabinet.

His stony silence was more disconcerting than his anger. Alinda studied his shrewd profile as he adjusted the flame. Even though his expression was blank, as if he had already put the incident behind him, she had the feeling he possessed a keenness that kept him a step ahead of most men.

His hair, the misty color of a golden dawn, was the antithesis to his controlled features. In windblown disarray, it curled thickly around his ears and the collar of his chambray shirt. His Levi's fit snugly, molding the sinewy strength of his legs when he moved to the table with two mugs of steaming coffee.

"Do you take anything?"

"No." She followed his cue and sat down at the wooden table.

"You're early," he said flatly.

"I didn't have a key to the main house." She never knew blue eyes to be so discerning, sifting through her superficial excuse and honing in on the truth after one look at her face. "Your door was open. I didn't think you would mind if I waited." She squirmed in her seat and her thick braid brushed across her breast.

His chair leg squeaked against the floor in protest as he moved to stand, suddenly restless. "Bring your cup. I'll walk you back." Nolan locked the door behind him this time. "I was on my way out. I had to stop at the barn and pick up some tools. That's when I saw you take the path to my place."

"Why didn't you just holler at me?"

He only shrugged, leaving Alinda feeling very uneasy. What happened to the congenial person she had spoken with on the telephone? She wondered. Did he suspect her motives already? Was she *that* transparent? Or was he just very adept at reading people? Alinda continued to follow Nolan along the narrow dirt-packed trail. The wind had come up and it whipped a few strands of hair loose from her french braid. She brushed them off her cheek and decided to be honest with him, at least partially. "I'd like to talk to you about the ranch, Mr. Taylor."

He was silent for a minute and she wasn't sure if he had heard her.

"I'm short two men today and there's a fence down at the north pasture." He unlocked the door and held it open for her. "I'll be back as soon as we get finished."

"Fine." She strolled through the quiet house, alone, memories pushing all thoughts of Nolan Taylor out of her mind. In the kitchen, she heard Jackson telling the cook how he wanted his eggs. In the study she saw his tall, slender body in the leather desk chair. It had been almost a year since he had been here, but she could still smell the cigars. She opened a window and inhaled the early summer breeze and gave in to a yawn. She kicked her shoes off, adjusted the pillows and stretched out on the camelback sofa. Overcome with exhaustion, she fell asleep quickly for the first time in weeks.

The sun was a faint diffuse glow through the west window when Alinda opened her eyes. She sat up instantly, her heart pounding furiously when she spotted a movement in her peripheral vision. "Did it ever occur to you to knock?" she demanded, blinking the sleep from her eyes.

"No more than it did you," he countered.

"I did knock," she said defensively.

His hair was damp and Alinda could smell the fresh scent of soap and water that lingered on his skin as he moved to stand over her. She felt a momentary sense of panic as his eyes narrowed.

"So did I," he countered with infuriating calm. He couldn't help but derive a small amount of pleasure from the heightening color in her cheeks. It left him to wonder if the pink tint was caused by being caught in a lie or from something else.

"I passed through town on my way back and picked up some groceries for you." The less she was seen around the area, he had reasoned, the safer he would be. A woman as attractive as Alinda Sterling would definitely cause heads to turn and tongues to wag, especially in a small town like this.

"Thank you." She eyed him speculatively. Why would he do something so kind after the threats she had made? Deciding two could play at catching more flies with honey . . . "I was so tired from the drive that food never entered my mind. But I think the fresh air has given me an appetite."

"Good." He held a hand out to help her from the sofa and smiled when she tried to cover a yawn. "It seems the fresh air has done more than make you hungry."

Two steps into the kitchen, Alinda screamed, "Ohhh!" and backed up into Nolan's rock-hard frame. His hands stole around her, his body coiling to shield and turn her away.

Preparing for the worst, his whole body tensed, ready to spring. With a trained eye, he searched the kitchen in one quick sweeping motion. Finding nothing amiss, he looked down questioningly at the woman huddled against him.

"A mouse!" She gestured with her arm in the direction she had seen the little creature scurry. She wiggled in Nolan's protective grip and said, "Do something."

He straightened, angry at Alinda for causing the fierce pounding in his chest over a creature that was more frightened of her than she was of it. "God, woman. You scared me half to death." Then she turned, and he experienced an unnerving shaft of desire as her breasts heaved against his chest. He dropped his hold on her as if suddenly burned, cursing under his breath. In a matter of seconds, this woman, whom he hardly knew, had made him feel the cold knife of fear and the hot shaft of desire, she had not only brooked his professional defenses, but his masculine ones as well.

"I'll get the broom," she said tartly.

He caught her arm, his lean fingers halting her progress, and laughed wryly. "And do what with it? It's probably halfway to China by now after that scream of yours." He walked around her. "I'll take care of the cooking if you think you can get it together to find us some plates and utensils."

Absently, she rubbed the flesh his hand had captured before cautiously following his instructions, one eye on the corner where the mouse had disappeared and the other eye on the man that kept a watchful eye on her.

The aroma of the small steaks under the broiler, topped with fresh sautéed mushrooms and rice, made Alinda's mouth water. "It looks delicious," she commented as he dished an equal amount on each plate. After the first bite, she complimented him again, somewhat grudgingly after his snide remark about her ability to set the table. "You're a very good cook." She shook a dash of salt on her steak. "Did you get the fence mended?"

He cut his steak in square chunks and nodded. "Had to. We've got over fifty heifers in there."

"Did you work on a ranch before you came here?"

"When I was a young man."

"Where?"

"All over," he said before taking a long pull of his beer.

"I had no idea what ranch life was like until Jackson

33

bought Indian Paintbrush. To be honest, I wasn't thrilled with the idea."

"Why?"

She liked the way he leaned forward; it lent a genuine interest to his inquiry. But was this easy camaraderie designed to throw her off? Was he hoping to find out something to use against her? "I suppose I saw it as a threat," she answered honestly, but cautiously as she piled a bite of fluffy rice onto her fork. "He only had one business, but he had a dozen hobbies. Of course, being a good friend, I'm sure you knew that," she goaded.

"I wouldn't call a cattle ranch this size a hobby."

"I know. It's an investment. I also know he bought it because it was a challenge. The owner was about to go bankrupt and it was an area Jackson had never ventured into." Alinda dropped her fork onto the empty plate and leaned back. "I thought it would take up what little free time we had left together."

"Did it?"

"Yes." Their glances locked for a few seconds and she was struck by his quiet watchfulness. By revealing something about herself and Jackson, she had hoped to learn a little about Nolan Taylor. She had failed. Looking into his deep-set blue eyes, she knew the wheels inside his head were spinning as quickly as hers, yet the expression on his face led her no closer to the truth of the situation than his spoken words.

"Want to flip for dish duty?" he asked, jarring the pensive expression on her face to one of mild surprise.

Unable to remember the last time she had washed a dish, she smiled.

It was a smile that brought a smile in response, totally unbidden, from the deepest part of him. "It's real simple," he said as if reading her thoughts. "I'll show you how."

"Really, Mr. Taylor. There's no need to make fun of me." She stood and cleared her place. "I know how to wash dishes."

Her back was to him, her shoulders erect. He wanted to run his hand down the length of her stiff spine and feel it relax beneath his fingers. She was a woman that stirred something in him, something alien and strange. Trouble.

"You cooked. It's only fair that I clean up."

He surprised her by agreeing. "I'll make the coffee."

"When did you meet Jackson?" she asked after the table was cleared and the sink was filled with sudsy water.

"He didn't tell you?" He asked, trying to stall. He knew she was going to eventually ask him some very pointed questions and for some reason he didn't want to have to lie to her.

Alinda shook her head, biting back the sarcastic retort that rose to her lips as she put the last dish in the drainer and dried her hands.

"Almost two years ago," he finally said, handing her a cup of black coffee and motioning for her to precede him into the den.

"I already know that!" Her temper flared despite her determination to remain emotionless. "How? Where? Do I have to pull it out of you?" She sat down in a vivid orange wingback chair, a perfect backdrop for her glossy black hair and the snapping obsidian eyes. Her legs crossed naturally at her ankles as her arms rested on the upholstery.

"He was in a plane that went down just south of the Colorado border in the San Juan Mountains of New Mexico." Nolan picked up a piece of pottery and examined it until he saw Alinda fidget in her chair. He then studied her with an intensity that made the air crackle with electricity. He had to decide how much to tell her. He couldn't afford an explosive, not to mention newsworthy, court battle. But if he told her the truth—he stood to lose even more. He replaced the ashtray without making a sound. "I saw it go down."

Confusion was written in the knit of her brow. Alinda shook her head. "Why didn't Jackson ever mention it? Why didn't you mention it at the lawyer's office?"

His mouth crooked into a wry slant, as he shrugged his shoulders.

Still too perturbed at the turn of the conversation to be anything but honest, she admitted, "It doesn't make sense." Nothing seemed to be making any sense lately, she thought.

"I was camping in the mountains."

There were still missing pieces to the puzzle. Suddenly, she remembered a particularly stirring nightmare Jackson had had several months after the crash. He had seemed to be reliving the episode all over again in his dream, sporadically mumbling and talking aloud. When Alinda had questioned him the next day, he wouldn't discuss it and told her he didn't remember the dream.

She had always thought his reticence to discuss the incident was because it had been such a frightful experience. Was it because he had something to hide? Had he been blackmailed into changing his will? She shuddered inwardly. There had to be another explanation. In those few nightmarish moments Jackson must have unknowingly revealed part of the real truth. She struggled to piece some of the events together and confronted Nolan with the little bit she remembered. "Somebody pulled him from that plane before it burst into flames. Was it you?"

There was a millisecond of surprise in his eyes, but he didn't confirm or deny her conclusions. Instead, his light eyebrow rose over his eye in a natural arch, his amused expression hiding his very serious thoughts. He felt certain her statement was only a suspicion because he was sure Jackson would have never broken his promise of silence. Nolan was going to have to tread lightly. Alinda Sterling was far more perceptive than he had given her credit for. He finally nodded. His shoulders slumped as he thrust his hands in his pockets, stretching the fabric of his jeans across his flat abdomen.

He felt old and tired and wondered if it was all worth it as he turned his back on the eyes that seemed to look straight through him. He had already been here longer than he had planned. It was probably time to move on anyway, he told himself. He wondered where he would spend the next six months or so. *Damn!* He had thought this would be the perfect place to hide when Jackson had made the offer and now that he only had six months or so to go this woman was throwing a wrench in his plans.

An idea dawned suddenly to Nolan and he mulled it over as he absently lit a cigarette and took a long drag from it. *Yes!* She just might go for it, he thought as he crushed out the cigarette and crossed the room to stand in front of her.

"I'll make you a deal, Mrs. Sterling. You give me six months and I'll be on my way. I'll leave you a smooth-running ranch that's firmly in the black. In return you promise not to press your claim to Indian Paintbrush."

He hated to beg—it went against him and everything he had ever stood for—but his life could depend on her answer. His hard jaw tightened further, the muscle work-

37

ing furiously as he decided to press the issue. "Six months, Mrs. Sterling. That's all I ask."

"I can't hide the fact that I'm surprised," she admitted, feeling immense relief because her blackmail hypothesis went out the window. If he had wanted the ranch bad enough to blackmail Jackson to get it, surely he wouldn't readily give it up? Had her imagination been working overtime? Was Jackson's bequest simply a magnanimous gesture to show his gratitude to Mr. Taylor? Or did he think he could come up with a way to swindle her out of the ranch if he had enough time? Was she foolish to give him any quarter at all? What was so magical about six months? She figured that to be about the end of the year. Would the statute of limitation be up for some heinous crime he had committed?

Even if she discounted the blackmail theory, there were still a number of unanswered questions. Why hadn't Jackson confided in her about the way he had survived the crash and why did Nolan turn up to run the ranch? Was it coincidence or had Jackson contacted him?

Then, there was this new twist—his cavalier attitude with the ranch. It aroused her curiosity even more. "You're willing to give up Indian Paintbrush, just like that?" Her hand waved carelessly in midair as skepticism replaced her surprise. "As long as I consent to let you stay here for six months?"

"I learned a long time ago that there are many more precious things in this life than material goods."

His eyes clouded, convincing Alinda that there was another side to this man, a side that no one had been close to in a long time, except maybe Jackson. Had he understood Nolan Taylor? Or just been intrigued, as she was? Had he come to Indian Paintbrush because it provided acres and acres in which to hide? And, if so, why

38

was he so willing to give it up? What was he afraid of? She shook herself out of the reverie. "You've got a deal Mr. Taylor." But only for now, she added silently.

Nolan didn't question her change of heart. His mind was already racing ahead, wondering whether it might be a good idea to encourage her to stay so he could keep an eye on her, or if he would be better off if she went back to Tulsa—out of sight, out of mind. But in her case, he seriously doubted that the tenet would apply. "You can stay here as long as you like," he offered. "I'm planning to stay in the foreman's cabin."

"You don't want to move in here?" He was definitely an enigma. Why would he choose the cramped cabin over the opulent main house?

"I never thought Jackson would leave this ranch to me. I want you to believe that." Curiously, it was important to him.

She sipped at the cold coffee and watched him over the cup's rim. Yes, she believed his story, what little he had revealed to her. There was a genuine quality about his mannerisms, a truthfulness in his eyes that defined his honesty more clearly than any tangible evidence ever could. But was she worldly enough to be that good a judge of character?

"I do believe you and thank you for your offer. It's very kind after the way I acted in Robert's office."

"We all say things we don't mean when we're under a strain." He shrugged and set his empty cup down and strolled to the window. The night was dark and still, reminding him of her dark eyes challenging him yet stirring his protective instincts at the same time. The stars were numerous and bright, twinkling as Alinda's eyes must have been before this tragedy.

The fishing should be good tomorrow, he thought. He

39

glanced back at the raven-haired woman. The wing of the chair cradled her head and her dark lashes fluttered against her ivory cheeks. She was incredibly fragile-looking, tired. She needed fresh air and sunshine to put the glow back in her features. He wondered how long she would stay here at Indian Paintbrush. God knew he was starving for a woman's company, but he had gone hungry before and he could do it again. In a way, it was ludicrous to encourage her to stay, and yet if he kept her busy, it would lessen her opportunities to talk to anyone else. He couldn't afford to let her stir up curiosity. This close-knit community thrived on gossip. If she went back to Tulsa, she just might be tempted to solicit some sort of help from a friend.

Damned if you do and damned if you don't. Wasn't that how the saying went?

He finally decided, as he turned to look at her, that he would rather have an adversary where he could keep an eye on her. He would begin by thinking of activities they could do together.

The cup slipped a fraction of an inch and dangled precariously from her fingers. Quickly, gently, he removed it from her delicate hand. Her eyelids drifted upward and she smiled at him, a lazy, unguarded smile that seemed to sap her remaining strength.

"I must have dozed off. You'll have to excuse me."

"It's late. No need for apologies." He picked up his hat from the end table and pulled the brim between his fingers, unaware that the simple gesture revealed the agitation within him. He was at the door, his hand on the brass knob, when he found himself turning back to face Alinda. "I'm going fishing in the morning. Would you like to come?" This way he could watch her and keep her away from the ranch at the same time.

40

Without hesitating, she answered, "I'd love it."

"You might not love it so much when I tell you what time I want to leave."

She made a show of bracing herself against the back of the sofa, her breasts thrust out and her head turned to one side. "Hit me with it."

He sucked in his breath at the provocative position she so unwittingly presented. "Five."

The back of her hand flew to her forehead, feigning a dizzy spell. "A.M.?"

He exhaled another exhilarating laugh at her heroics and it felt good. He briefly explained why he wanted to get such an early start. "Still game?"

"Yes."

"I'll pick you up out front at five then."

"I'll look forward to it." When the door clicked behind Nolan, Alinda couldn't help but smile. He wasn't going to be such a tough nut to crack after all.

She unpacked her few necessities, laid out what she would wear in the morning and fell into bed, feeling quite confident. It had been a busy day and she was physically as well as mentally exhausted, but she had made progress. He had offered to let her stay and invited her to spend the morning with him. Tomorrow night, he would be telling her his life story. She wouldn't allow herself to deliberate on the consequences she might suffer once she found out his background.

41

CHAPTER THREE

The sky was a pearl gray, preparing for a new dawn as Nolan waited for Alinda. He leaned casually against the truck and his arms hung loosely at his sides with a cigarette burning between his fingers. But inside, he was coiled tighter than a python around its prey. What had made him do a fool thing like inviting her to go with him?

All his doubts were cleared from his mind like fine cobwebs during a late spring rain as the answer to his question came in the form of a tall, lithe woman lightly descending the porch steps. He told himself it was because he had to find out exactly what she was up to. The fact that she was a beautiful lady was a fringe benefit and no one knew better than he that he was due a few. He noticed that her hair floated loosely around her face; it was the first time he had seen her that it wasn't pulled back or twisted up. She was breathtaking even in an oversized shirt drawn in at the waist by tight-fitting jeans.

He straightened and tossed his cigarette to the gravel

drive. Her graceful, unrestrained beauty moved him more than any woman ever had, and he'd seen plenty. When she smiled up at him, causing the tiny hairs on his arms to rise in further awareness, he realized he hadn't seen everything—not yet anyway.

"Good morning. I brought some coffee and rolls." She swung the bag up on the seat in front of her.

He hadn't even noticed she was carrying a bag.

After giving her a boost on to the high seat, he asked, "All set?" Then he locked her in the cab.

Shafts of pink and yellow were sprouting across the horizon as they drove toward their destination. Alinda was thrilled to be able to sit back and enjoy the simplicity of a sunrise. She rolled the window down and let the cool morning breeze whip at her face, giving her cheeks a healthy pink glow. It was so peaceful, she could almost forget the real reason she was here. As much as she wanted to jump on Nolan Taylor, pummel his chest with her fist and demand that he tell her the truth, she had decided that luring him into a false sense of security was by far the more reasonable approach.

"Tell me again why we needed to get to the pond this early." She yawned. "And try to be convincing this time."

"We've had unusually warm weather for this time of year. Normally it's not this hot until later in July. The fish scavenge for food in the shallow water early in the morning or late in the evening while the water is still cool. Later in the day it's too hot and they move to the deeper parts of the pond."

"Why couldn't we sleep in and fish the deeper waters in the afternoon?" she persisted in teasing him.

"Because the bass would have already eaten while you

were lazing away and they wouldn't be as apt to bite in the afternoon for lack of appetite."

"Oh, right," as she covered another mock yawn.

"Your enthusiasm overwhelms me." A twitch of amusement pulled at the corners of his mouth. "How's that coffee of yours?"

Alinda poured them both a cup of coffee, careful to only fill the cups halfway, since they were traveling across an old dirt road. Nolan avoided the ruts with an assuredness that could only be born from the constant driving over it. They both were content to enjoy the early-morning quiet. The low purr of the engine and an occasional greeting from a cow that had wandered near the fenced roadside were the only intrusions.

"Is this still a part of Indian Paintbrush?"

"Yes." He stretched a muscular arm out, pointing to the east. "As the crow flies, the big house is only about twenty minutes from the pond."

They hit a deep rut and Alinda bounced out of her seat and back again. She set her empty cup down and buckled her seat belt. "How much farther is it?"

"Another mile or so." He glanced over at the death grip she had on the armrest. "I'm so used to it. I didn't think about it being this rough." They stopped on a rise and Nolan pointed to Alinda's window. "Maybe that will make it worth the ride."

There, nestled in a valley, was a winding pond that flowed almost as far as the eye could see. "It's lovely," Alinda commented as she alighted from the truck.

Nolan lifted the fishing tackle and rods from the bed of the truck and held an elbow out for Alinda as they went down the slight incline toward the pond. It was a blend of grass-lined banks, overhanging willow trees along one shore, a small inlet stream and a deep side at a small dam.

While he was preparing the lines, Nolan said, "If you're not too tired when we're through fishing, I'll walk you over the dam to that knoll." He nodded at a tree-lined hill to the south and waited until Alinda had spotted it before continuing. "On the other side of that grove of trees there's an excellent view of the ranch proper."

He made a few casts, reeling it in very slowly each time. He seemed totally wrapped up in the task, which allowed Alinda to observe him in the relaxed atmosphere. He was quite handsome; she also sensed that, beneath the bravado, there was a softness—the kind of softness that did not belong to criminals. She felt an instant pang of guilt for hiring the detective, but as quickly pushed it to the back of her mind when Nolan handed the rod to her.

He picked up another rod and walked several feet away. From the corner of her eye, Alinda watched him make a few casts, then retrieve it with ease from the maze of willow branches. It didn't look hard.

She tried it, pushing the button and snapping the rod back and then forward. When her line didn't fly back overhead to plunk into the water, as Nolan's had, she turned around with a certain amount of trepidation. The glittery worm dangled from a tree limb not too far behind her.

She glanced at Nolan who had wandered even farther down the bank, still casting and reeling. Alinda walked over to stand directly beneath the artificial bait. With her eyes shut and two fingers crossed, she tugged on the line, hoping it would fall out on its own. Then with growing frustration, she yanked on it. When that didn't work, she found a foothold and hoisted herself up to the branch that held her line.

"What are you doing?" His laughter burst from his lungs at the picture she made straddling the limb.

"My hook caught in the tree."

His hands spanned her small waist to safely help her to the ground. "I know I should have asked this sooner, but do you know how to cast?"

Alinda bit her lower lip. "It wasn't exactly a requirement of graduation at the boarding school I attended."

"Have you ever been fishing?"

She shook her head repentantly.

"Why didn't you tell me?"

"I was afraid you wouldn't take me."

It was his turn to shake his head. "Let's go back to the bank and I'll give you a few pointers." He took their poles in one hand and clasped Alinda's in his other. "The first rule is to look behind you to make sure the coast is clear. This time it was the tree, next time, it could be me." He eyed her with mock severity.

Nolan stood behind her, his arms circling her and positioning her hands properly on the rod. "It's all in your wrist." His large hand swallowed her slender wrist and moved it back and forth in a snapping motion. "Let's say you want to try around that stump. Just aim your rod. You want to drop your worm far enough past your target so that you don't scare the fish." Still holding her braced against his torso, he showed her how to let the line out and they watched it sail fifteen feet past the stump. "Then slowly, reel your line back in." When the worm was back at the tip of her rod, Nolan said, "Now, you try it."

The transparent line went whistling, not dropping quite as far out as Nolan's cast.

"Good, but try to remember that the fish are more than likely up in four or five feet of water, so try to throw

46

the line at about a thirty-degree angle. That way it travels along the shallow water a little longer."

Alinda tried again. Almost past the stump again, something grabbed her hook. "I have something!" she cried excitedly.

Nolan quickly jerked the line to set the hook and instructed Alinda to reel it in. She was pulled forward, as the fish ran with her line, all the way to the water's murky edge before Nolan wrapped her in the protection of his arms. "You planning on swimming with it?"

She laughed nervously. The line sang with tension, then slackened as the big fish jumped out of the water, arching and extending its scaled length. Alinda reeled as fast as she could. The tip of her rod bowed and vibrated with the bass's fight for freedom. Several minutes later Alinda had finally won and the fish was flipping on the grassy bank.

"Nice, Ali. Real nice." Nolan held the fish up by its mouth. "It's a black bass. I'd say about three pounds."

She was surprised at the flood of warmth she felt when he had so endearingly shortened her given name. It was a little unnerving. No one in her family or her circle of friends had ever done that. They were always very formal. "I want to try it again," she said, attributing her excitement solely to catching her first fish.

Nolan chuckled, working to free the hook from the bass's mouth. "Go for it," he told her once the line dangled loose. He put the fish on the empty stringer already secured by a stake in the ground and tossed it out far enough for the fish to be under water.

He watched her cast a few times and then picked up his own rod and moved several yards away from her, smiling to himself, indulgent and mystified all at the same time. He would've never guessed the extent of her enthusiasm. After all, she was a very rich lady. From the time she was born, she had been given everything she could dream of and here she was on the banks of a muddy cow pond fishing with an eighteen-dollar rod.

An hour later he could just barely make out her slender figure on the point of the cove, shifting restlessly from one foot to the other. He followed her line. It was hung in a clump of stumps and brush twenty yards out. He reeled in his line, silently cursing it for the lack of even a nibble and grateful for an excuse to be near her again. He made his way back to Alinda, a complacent feeling spreading through him.

When he approached her, she faced him with a distressed expression. "I'm sorry. I can't seem to get it loose."

"Happens to the best of us." He tugged at her line a few times himself without success, then pulled some clippers from his pocket. "I'll just cut it off. I've got plenty of extras."

"I still feel terrible. I'll buy you another one."

Nolan looked up at her, his brows knit together. "No. I have plenty."

"That fish," she pointed to the black bass, its iridescent scales gleaming in the shallow depths. "It was near that stump so I thought I would try there again."

"Sounds logical. I probably would've done the same thing."

"But there's so much brush and debris, I should've known better. I don't have the expertise to keep from getting tangled up."

Nolan laughed. "Not even a pro has *that* much expertise. Getting hung up is just a hazard of the sport of bass fishing."

He dug around in his tackle box. "Instead of a worm, I'll put a spinnerbait on here."

Alinda leaned over to see just what a spinnerbait looked like.

"It doesn't hang up as easily as the worm." He handed her the rod and then changed his own to a buzz bait. "I think all that squealing you did when you caught that three-pounder scared all the other fish to cover in deep water."

She looked crestfallen. "Do you think so?"

He grinned as he shook his head, thinking he had smiled more in the past twenty-four hours than he had in years. She made it too easy to forget that with a few well-placed phone calls, she could put an end to him.

"Oh!" She frowned at him in mock indignation.

They were standing very close. The faint scent of her perfume wafted to Nolan's nostrils and there was the warm glow of a smile on her unpainted mouth. The urge to kiss her lips, tinged pink by the morning's sun, an unknowing but nonetheless inviting look in her eyes, was more than he could resist. His head bent to capture her mouth before she could read his mind and slip away. Her lips were smooth, like tide-polished pebbles, yet pliant as warm sand, molding and giving beneath the firmness of his own. "Ali," he whispered against her lips.

He had never known such raw need. His hands ached to hold her and mold her feminine figure against him, but he forced himself to go slow even though blood was rushing through his every beating pulse, pounding its way to his core.

His mouth lifted and he unhurriedly studied the quivering heart-shaped curves that had formed a perfect seal against his own, then traced her lips with his thumb. Time stopped, leaving only the two of them alone with nature's elements. Like the iridescent lure and the mighty black bass, the stronger was unable to resist the temptation of the weaker for even one more tantalizing moment. Nolan tilted his head to the side and there in the morning sunshine, he brought their lips together again. In that instant the stronger knew he had been hooked. They were more confusing than any kisses he had ever known before. He wanted them to go on forever, to drown himself in this swirling depth of emotion. He was very tender, careful to feel her acceptance, but as his tongue ventured to taste the sweetness of hers, she pulled away.

Alinda's fingers bit into Nolan's shoulders and forced some distance between them. Her hand flew to her lips, moist and trembling, as her head shook violently from side to side, the gravity of what had taken place pressing in on her with leaden force.

"Ali." His blue eyes were pleading with her.

She turned and fled to the truck, her thoughts in a riotous state. She searched the heavens, fully expecting Jackson to be looking down on her. It didn't matter that she didn't see his physical presence because she felt him there with every fiber of her being.

"Alinda?" His voice was firmer now, not so tortured.

She jumped at the commanding tone. "Please take me back."

"I know what you're thinking . . ."

"Don't you dare presume to know what I'm thinking!" Haughty anger was the only barrier between her and the tears burning her eyes.

Nolan slammed the door after she was safely inside and they made the entire drive in silence. After what seemed an absolute eternity they parked in front of the big house. Alinda bounded out of her side. Blinded by her tears, she stumbled on the steps but quickly righted herself. She went to the den because the room had always vibrated with Jackson's presence. She inhaled deeply, searching for the fine aroma of his favorite tobacco. She ran her hand over the tooled leather chair and then along the cold rock mantle of the fireplace. She closed her eyes, willing his image to fill her mind, but the one that came clearly focused was tall and bronzed, blond hair blowing in the cool summer breeze.

"He's dead, Ali." His voice was quiet, but its huskiness pulsed across the room.

"Not . . . in . . . my heart." The sobs were wrenching and painful. Her hand was a fist at her breast.

"Nor in mine."

"I loved him! I truly did."

"I know, but you can't stop living simply because he has. Life goes on. You can give it meaning or you can bury yourself alive in memories." She was vulnerable and yet so incredibly sensual. He had never had such an overwhelming urge to protect and make love at the same time.

"I haven't stopped living. I just don't need casual sex to be complete. Don't you see that would make a mockery of what Jackson and I shared? I just buried him three and a half months ago."

"I wasn't speaking of sex. I was thinking more of love, warmth, and companionship. Don't you think he loved you enough to want that for you?" His voice was deep, yet intensely soft.

She was so confused. Was she frustrated by the fact that she was drawn to a man so soon after Jackson's death or because she had reacted in an intensely physical way to Nolan Taylor, a man who might have swindled Jackson out of a half a million dollars, and maybe worse?

Nolan took a hesitant step toward her, wanting to

51

gather her in his arms and cradle her tear-stained face against his chest. He had an overwhelming urge in the pit of his stomach, a need to console and be consoled by this woman. He had not lost a loved one, but something just as precious to him—his freedom.

When her body tensed with anxiety at his advance, he stopped in midstride. His normally poker-faced features screwed up in disgust with himself for not being able to control his longing for her. *Damn!* Not only was he putting her in danger, but himself as well.

CHAPTER FOUR

After watching the play of emotions on Nolan's face, Alinda felt nothing but relief when he turned to leave. And damn him anyway! She had had fun this morning. Fun! She had almost forgotten the meaning of the word. Why did he have to ruin it? Why did he force her to question her own feelings, to probe sensitive emotions that were still so close to the surface?

Sniffing, she wiped away the tears, her fingers delicately skimming across her still-weepy eyes and the graceful slope of her cheekbones.

Long, determined strides took her out of the dark, masculine atmosphere of the study and down the stuffy hallway to the bedroom. The morning had become sultry. She raised the window and stood there, face upturned, to let the breeze circulate around her tear-stained face and tense neck and shoulders. Her red-rimmed eyes closed and she breathed deeply, inhaling the sweet scent of honeysuckle. Damp wisps of hair clung to her neck when she left the warm breeze to retrieve her bag from the musty closet. She sneezed as the dust drifted from the top shelf and settled around her. The house needed to be thoroughly cleaned and aired out before she came again. Why would she ever come back? It was only habit that she thought of cleaning. She had no intention of ever returning, not as long as Nolan Taylor was here, anyway.

Hastily, she began folding the few things she had unpacked and collected her toiletries from the bathroom. She had no desire to see Nolan Taylor again, therefore the sooner she was away from the ranch, the better. He was a rogue with no scruples. He had proven it, beyond a shadow of a doubt, this morning. She had already agreed not to contest the will. Did he think she was so sexually starved that one kiss would seal the bargain, cause her hormones to overrule her head, just in case she should entertain any thoughts of changing her mind? Tossing her night clothes into the bag, she decided to leave the detective work to the professionals, as she should have done in the beginning.

Nolan stood in the doorway of the barn with his feet spread apart and knees locked, unconcerned by the bantam hen clucking as she flitted from the stack of hay beside him. His face was expressionless, but his insides were being eaten alive. His grip tightened on the pitchfork and, he threw it, one-handed, spearing a stack several feet away. He had set a match to an already volatile situation. What would she do now? Would she stick with her promise to let Jackson's will stand?

He wasn't even conscious that he had moved toward the car until he saw Alinda's eyes, huge doe eyes caught in the sight of a hunter's rifle, staring at him through the reflection of the rearview mirror. Were they rounded in fear . . . or disgust? They cut to his very soul but he took another step forward, wondering what he could say to her. But he didn't have to worry. He saw her frantically trying to insert the key into the ignition and immediately halted.

If he was smart he would leave today, not wait around to find out what her plans were. Brushing the hair off his forehead and wiping the back of his neck with a red bandanna, he tried desperately to blame the hollowness he felt on something other than the woman sending dust clouds up as she accelerated away. He thought of the way her tender lips had been so pliant against his and his jaw clenched, his heart tightened so, it almost quit beating. He turned and strode angrily toward the house. He could use a drink. After all, it was *his* liquor and *his* house, whether she liked it or not.

The empty expanse of gray highway ahead of Alinda brought a surge of loneliness almost as severe as the one she had suffered immediately after Jackson's death. What was happening to her? One minute she felt wonderfully alive and the next, guilty and ashamed.

One hand left the steering wheel and touched her lips. In reality, she knew she deserved part of the blame. The kiss had truly surprised her, but it was her own response that she found utterly appalling. She had been cold for so long and Nolan Taylor had warmed her, warmed her to her very core with one kiss. She could not deny the truth. It had been over a year since she had been kissed like that. The emotional pain that arced from her chest to her throat was more intense than any physical blow could be. How could she have let him kiss her—and worse, stood there, a willing participant?

Two weeks later, Alinda was still no closer to an answer even though she had asked herself the question a dozen times over. She traversed the long hallway, passing the closed door to Jackson's study, then turned back to go in. Everything was exactly the same. Her hand fluttered to her throat. Breathing heavily, she scrambled out, shut the door, and leaned against it. There was still so much of him in there, giving her the eerie feeling he had only left for a moment, not for a lifetime. Oh, God, she had loved him so!

Breathing heavily, she reached for the doorknob one more time. She was going to reach out for that third step of grieving—acceptance. If she waited for it to come to her, she was afraid she would hide from it forever. Until her arrival at Indian Paintbrush, she knew that she was pretending it hadn't happened. And until Nolan had kissed her, she had refused to even weep for her loss. But it was time to face reality. There was no one to take care of Alinda Sterling but Alinda Sterling herself. The time had come to face her future head on.

In a show of determination, she jerked the drapery cord. The sun streaked through the window, harsh shafts of yellow light illuminating the rich burgundy leather chairs and the fine grain of polished cherry wood. She let her fingers run along the carved edge of the desk, lingering on memories before removing the papers from a safe hidden behind a paneled wall. She sat down at the desk and thumbed through the stack of business papers, then more slowly she went through the personal papers, suddenly realizing she was searching for something, anything that would give her a clue to Nolan Taylor.

There were insurance policies, bank statements, deeds to real estate properties in several states, and oil leases in Texas and Oklahoma, but nothing at all about the mysterious Mr. Taylor.

She leaned back with a sigh, eyeing the sorted stacks of

paper covering the desk top. At this moment, she wished that Jackson hadn't scoffed at having a personal secretary. It would have made all of this much easier.

It had been a long day. The window was barely letting in enough light to see by, but before she quit, there was one more thing Alinda had to take care of. She punched out Jan's number on the telephone hidden in the wood-grained box.

"Hi. How are your plans for the benefit going?" Alinda asked after her sister's friendly hello. "I've decided to help."

"I was hoping you would. I need all the help I can get."

Alinda shook her head in consternation. As usual, her sister was unashamedly honest. "Why do you volunteer for these positions?"

"Because when you're the chairperson, you only have to organize. I'm great at that," Jan beamed in her typically confident fashion.

"You have a point. When is the first meeting?"

"Next Thursday at ten."

"All right. And Jan, thanks for including me."

"I owe you the thanks."

"You better hold off on the thanks until you hear my ideas," Alinda warned teasingly. "See you next week."

Leaning heavily on the highly polished banister, she trudged up the curved staircase and felt an overwhelming urge to sit down and rest before she reached the landing. Reflecting on the past two weeks, she felt she had accomplished a great deal. She had settled most of the fine details of the will, sold Jackson's automobiles and had come to an agreement with his business partners about the running of the company. She was no longer emotionally drained, only physically exhausted, she thought with a rueful smile.

She showered and readied herself for bed. Ambivalence was a miserable emotion, she decided as she pulled the covers up to her chest. How could she love Jackson so deeply, and yet still be attracted to a man she had spent so little time with?

She still knew nothing at all about Nolan Taylor's background. Robert had hired two different detectives and neither one had been able to come up with anything concrete. For all she knew, he could be an escaped convict, a murderer, or—she could go on and on, but what was the point? She was still drawn to him in a way that was both alarming and exciting at the same time. The more she tried to put him out of her mind, the more she thought of him. In a song, there was always a verse that reminded her of him. In a crowd, there was a tall, blond head that she expected to be him and never was. And when she drifted off into a fitful sleep, he was there waiting for her, in her dreams.

Alinda awoke with a start in the wee hours of morning. She wasn't sure what had disturbed her until thunder clapped frighteningly close. She pulled the covers around her and tried to go back to sleep, but something bothered her. The night noises were different somehow.

She slid her feet into satin slippers and crossed to the window. A quiet gasp escaped her lips. Rain pelted the panes of glass and the water rushing down the street turned it into a swiftly moving river.

The house sat on top of a rise so she wasn't too worried about flooding, but she wanted to check all the same. She picked up her satin wrap from the end of the bed and draped it around the matching gown. Another clap of thunder rumbled as she reached the stairway and she shook with apprehension. Halfway down the richly carpeted steps, the lights went out. "Dammit!" Carefully, she felt her way down each step and when she opened the kitchen door, Mary was there holding a lit candle that cast a creepy flickering shadow on the copper pots.

"Don't we have any flashlights?" Alinda asked.

"Yes, I keep a big one in the pantry. That's where I was headed when the lights went out." Mary moved past Alinda, her quilted robe giving her a bulky shape in the semidarkness.

"Is a radio with batteries too much to ask for?"

"Also in the pantry," Mary answered with a nod.

Alinda took the flashlight and pointed it out several windows downstairs while Mary found a station on the radio.

"The rosebushes are totally under water," she announced with dismay as she joined Mary at the table. "Have you heard anything yet?"

"Several major streets are flooded and a number of apartment complexes have been evacuated. They must be using boats. The water is more than six feet high at several major intersections."

"That's hard to believe."

The disc jockey mentioned Haskell County and Alinda's ears perked up. "That's where the ranch is located."

The news was bleak. Alinda realized that her concern was more for Nolan than for the ranch. But he was a human being. That was only natural, wasn't it?

"The rain seems to be letting up. I think I'll try to get some sleep." The housekeeper stood. "Unless you need me for something else?"

"You go ahead. I'm going to wait for another report."

As soon as Mary had left the kitchen Alinda wound

her robe sash between her fingers, alternately wrinkling and stretching the fabric. By dawn, she had paced a circle around the kitchen, in the dark, the candle long since burned out in its silver dish. The six o'clock news reports were not good either. The death and injured toll mounted every hour as rescue crews scoured the countryside. Haskell and McIntosh counties were among the hardest hit by the storm. She went to the study and located Nolan's number, then picked up the phone and unexpectedly, the line was dead. She dropped it back in its cradle with an oath of frustration. Why hadn't she thought of that?

Back in the kitchen Alinda found Mary poaching eggs on the gas stove top. "The phone lines are out."

"Want some hot tea?" Mary asked.

Alinda nodded. "I'm worried. The radio said it's one of those one-hundred-year rains. The eastern and southern parts of the state were the hardest hit."

"Crews are probably already out repairing the phones and the electricity." Mary crossed the room and spooned the eggs onto a serving dish. "The water has receded a lot. I looked out when I got up."

The housekeeper's words did not alleviate Alinda's anxiety.

After breakfast, she bathed, arranged her hair in a loose bun at her crown, added a light shading of blush to her high cheekbones, a swipe of pink-tinted gloss to her lips and dressed at a faster pace than usual.

Late in the morning some of the local lines were finally repaired. Alinda was notified by the ringing of her own phone, startling her after the long silence. "Hello."

"Are you all right over there?"

"I'm fine, Jan. You all?"

"We're okay. The car was washed three blocks down

60

the street by high water, but there's no water in the house."

"At least you're all safe; the car can be replaced."

"True," Jan agreed.

"Just so you won't worry, I want you to know if I can't reach the ranch in a few hours, I'm driving to it after my story hour this afternoon. That area was hit hard by the storm. I might be able to help." She thought of the damage high winds could do to the horses and cattle, the forty-year-old house and barns, not to mention Nolan. Despite the dangerous weather, she knew he would have been out trying to save the animals.

"Alinda, I know you're worried, but it's really not your concern anymore."

Jan was right, of course. Legally, it really wasn't her concern. Emotionally, it was all she could think about. "You're probably right, but I have to go."

"Indian Paintbrush is two hours from here. A lot of the roads were washed out. You probably won't even be able to get through. What if you get stranded?"

"I've got to try."

"I knew you would listen to reason," Jan said sarcastically, then muttered, "I don't know why I bothered."

"I appreciate your concern, Jan. I really do. This may be a moot point anyway. In all likelihood, the lines will be fixed by this afternoon."

"You'll be careful."

"Of course. Give the kids a hug for me." As soon as Alinda heard the dial tone, she punched out Nolan's number again, this time by memory. A high-pitched signal shrilled in her ear.

She glanced at her watch and knew she would have to hurry if she was going to make story hour on time.

The streets were a mess of stalled cars and debris. She

was fifteen minutes late and the children were full of questions about the storm, turning her usual two-hour visit into three and a half.

The drive home was a little quicker, but Alinda still would be leaving for Indian Paintbrush later than she would have liked.

After trying Nolan's number once more, she threw a few things in the suitcase, changed her wool slacks for jeans, and her suede pumps for practical leather boots, never stopping long enough to analyze her real reasons for the sudden trip.

On the drive to the ranch, doubts began pressing in on her. Twice she had had to double back and take an alternate route, once because of high water and another time because of a washed-out bridge. Through Haskell and finally Eufaula, the storm's path was clearly visible. Sludge and silt clung to the antiqued store fronts and covered the sidewalks. Cars had been washed off the road, muddy grass and debris covering them, evidence that they had been completely under water. Alinda drove slowly, surveying the damage. She had never seen anything like it.

When she turned, curving eastward onto Highway 9, her heart pounded faster and faster with every mile she covered. The rapid beat of her heart had nothing to do with the destruction of the storm, though. Whether Nolan would be happy to see her, or less than thrilled, was something she had not stopped to consider until now. She hadn't talked to him in over two weeks. And after the way they had parted, he might not welcome her presence at Indian Paintbrush, even though he had told her to consider it her home. He might have changed his mind.

She knew he was still at the ranch because of the detective's report last week, but the report had not revealed where he was sleeping. He might have decided to move into the main house, after all.

Well, you're about to find out, Alinda. At dusk, she pulled off the highway onto a road where muddy water deceivingly hid the potholes and was relieved to see the old house and grounds relatively unharmed. She noticed a few shingles missing from the roof as she parked the car in front of the main house. With her handbag slung over her shoulder, she climbed the few steps to the porch.

Her hand burrowed into her bag, searching for the key ring she had neglected to return. After several seconds of futilely sifting through the bag's contents, she gave up and tried the door. But it was securely bolted.

A flash of light sent an electrical charge from the dark cloud overhead to a nearby tree. Alinda gasped and covered her ears as the thunder cracked almost immediately. It began to drizzle again and she tugged her hat a little lower on her forehead. The canvas brim hid her ebony hair and kept the moisture off of her face. The untailored trench coat she wore protected the rest of her. She skirted the long screened-in porch and the berryless Nandina bushes. The screen door stood askew, another minor trace of damage to the property by the storm. She tried the doorknob, exhaling a sigh of relief when it turned easily and clicked open.

She stopped just outside the doorway when she noticed the broken window and the missing screen. Burglars or just the storm? she wondered nervously. After another step into the room, she noticed the faint glow from the bedroom at the far end of the house and wished the kitchen light were on as she stumbled over a strange object. She started to call out when an arm shot around from behind her and like a steel pipe pressed against her throat. It cut off all sound she so desperately tried to get out. She was close to panic when she realized it had also cut off her air supply.

Tears of shock and pain sprang into her eyes. It was a finely honed, hair-roughened forearm that hooked around her neck. She didn't have a chance against the masculine strength she felt pressed against her back. Her mind worked furiously as her nails bit into the muscular arm at her throat. She tried to think, tried to squelch the panic that continued to rise inside her like huge tidal waves. She forced herself to remember her self-defense course and somehow managed to summon up the maneuvers that the teacher had said may someday save her life.

CHAPTER FIVE

The dim room began to spin. The dark floor seemed to drop from beneath her feet. Breathing was a white-hot pain in her chest. She fought the urge to pass out, tried valiantly to remember the self-defense tactics. She raised her knee and with all the strength she could muster, Alinda rammed the bottom of her boot into the attacker's knee.

Her surprise maneuver threw him off balance, but not enough for Alinda to break completely free. He grabbed her wrist in a punishing grip and she spun around, pushing him away with all her might, kicking his boot-protected shin. She had the chance to look at him, but she couldn't, suddenly afraid that seeing his face would, in her terrified state, send her over the edge.

In the ensuing struggle, her hat sailed across the room and her hair tumbled around her shoulders. Alinda was wild with panic as they lost their balance and fell to the tiled floor, her attacker's hard body sprawled across her, knocking the breath from her burning lungs. She watched in horror as he very deliberately straddled her, covering her tense body with his. Rough hands went around her slender arms, pinning her writhing frame helplessly to the floor.

She realized she was the only one still fighting, her breathing heavy and hard to her ears. The atmosphere had changed and suddenly she wondered who was attacking whom. Her flailing limbs tentatively ceased their struggle, but remained tense and ready to strike at a moment's notice. His hold loosened, but he did not let her go. He loomed over her and she could feel the definite boldness of his arousal pressing into her thigh. She began to shake, his stillness more frightening than his violent attack.

Nolan hated himself for the sudden shaft of desire that bolted through him once he realized it was Ali's all too soft and feminine figure struggling beneath him. He gently forced her face up to meet his fierce gaze, unable to believe it was truly her until she opened her eyes. They widened simultaneously with his. Sparks of fleeting emotions arced between them. Surprise. Shock. Disbelief. Desire.

He stood quickly and then limped to the far side of the room, putting as much distance between them as possible. One minute he was cold and emotionless, struggling for his life and the next he was on fire, consumed with desire. Only she could do that to him. He flipped on the light and turned to face her with a grim expression.

"Mr. Taylor?"

"Good God, woman, are you trying to kill me or just make sure I never walk again?" Nolan demanded breathlessly.

"Only defending myself," she croaked, still wary.

"You do a damn good job of it, let me tell you!"

Alinda winced as she put pressure on her right ankle. "Are you hurt?"

The rolling of her huge obsidian eyes let him know how insincere his question appeared to be. "If I'm not, it'll be a small miracle."

Nolan walked toward her and slipped an arm around her waist for support. "Let me see," he commanded gruffly.

"No . . ." Eyeing him with trepidation, she wanted to protest, but her knees chose that particular time to buckle.

"Don't argue. You've caused enough trouble for one day."

"I've caused trouble?" She sputtered into a fit of coughing.

After helping her to the cane-bottom chair, he filled a glass of water and held it out to her. "Drink it." He removed her boot and his hands gingerly roamed over the injured ankle. One followed the smooth skin up her calf, the other gently twisted and rotated her very feminine foot. "It's not broken."

"Really, Mr. Taylor, I'm perfectly capable of deciding for myself." Her voice was raw, her throat burning as another fit of coughing caught her by surprise.

Nolan ran his hands up and down the seams of his jeans, impatient, anxious to know she was really unharmed. Mistaken identity or not, he couldn't believe he had treated someone so fragile with such violence. *Fragile?* She was a hellcat! He frowned inwardly, thinking she could certainly hold her own as he squatted in front of her and his bruised knee twinged with pain.

The taut fabric stretched across his thighs, making Alinda even more aware of his masculinity. She set the empty glass on the table and tried to ignore the pleasant burning sensation in her mid-section, the sensation that had obliterated her common sense a few short weeks ago when he had kissed her.

Very gently, he cradled her chin between his thumb and fingers, tilting her head to get a better look at her neck. His jaw clenched and his hand shook imperceptibly as he delicately moved her hair behind her shoulder. The angry red welt that slashed across her neck and shoulder were a startling contrast to her smooth ivory skin. He dropped his hands, annoyed with himself for jumping to the defense so quickly, and with her for showing up, totally unexpected.

"I thought you were a burglar. Why didn't you come through the front door? Or is it just a habit of yours to sneak in the back way?" His voice was tinged with sarcasm, a cover for his overwhelming guilt at how close he had come to really hurting her. His feelings for her were at such odds with his common sense, he didn't know whether he was coming or going.

When Alinda started to speak, he waved her off in a restless movement of his hand. "I'm sorry. Don't talk."

"I'm fine, really." She stood and put weight on her sore ankle to prove it. The way he continued to eye her with disdain compelled her to explain herself. "The front was locked and I couldn't find the key." She rolled her head around her shoulders, trying to ward off the stiffness setting in. "How's your knee?"

"I'll live. I'll be crippled the rest of my life, but I'll live," he grumbled testily.

Why had he jumped at her that way? What could he possibly be afraid of that drove him to attack a person with such violence? Was she crazy to even be alone with the man? And yet, when she thought of the way he had so delicately examined her leg and neck it was hard to believe he could have an unsavory past. But she chastised herself for being so trusting, reminding herself that the world was filled with unsuspecting victims.

She shivered and hoped he hadn't noticed. "If you greet all your guests like that, you probably don't get many visitors around here."

"I don't." His voice was bleak, its sheer emptiness echoing around the room. "Speaking of guests, to what do I owe your visit?"

"I was worried. The phones were out. I thought I might be able to help."

He looked at her dubiously. "Help? Doing what?"

His sharp words stung. It was obvious what he must think of her. "I could be very useful, given half a chance, Mr. Taylor."

"So you drove all the way down here just to—uh—check on things? This ranch must mean more to you than you let on."

His eyes were the most discerning blue Alinda had ever seen. Was that sarcasm in his tone or was he just so blunt that it seemed sarcastic? He was such a complex man. Was it all a game to him? This hide-and-seek attitude he constantly displayed?

"I'd like to stay a day or two if it's not an imposition . . ." Her voice dropped off, terribly uncomfortable under his scrutinizing gaze.

"You're certainly in no position to drive back today." He shrugged, seemingly indifferent. "Stay as long as you like. I'll be back in a few hours. I've got to go to Stigler for the glass to replace the window. Meanwhile, you keep the doors locked. There's been a lot of looting since the storm last night."

Alinda delicately cleared her throat. "Are you still living in the foreman's cabin?"

69

Nolan's nod was curt. "You may think me a lot of dastardly things, Mrs. Sterling, but I don't go back on my word. The main house is all yours."

When Nolan left, Alinda breathed a sigh of relief. She brought her bags in from the car and unpacked. Suddenly famished, she returned to the kitchen but found the cabinet and the refrigerator virtually empty. Her stomach growled in protest and she laughed out loud.

She made a trip to the small store fifteen miles from the ranch and purchased enough to last a few days. It took her but a few minutes to put everything away, smiling as she placed the last item, a fat frying chicken, in the meat drawer of the refrigerator. She had a special evening planned. If the way to a man's heart was through his stomach, so might be the trail to his past.

The gray drizzle of morning had given way to a sunny, sizzling afternoon. The moist ground almost steamed in the high humidity. Alinda decided to change into something cooler. She freshened her makeup and then twisted her hair into a loose knot before walking out to the backyard, barefoot, to cool off in the shade of a large mimosa tree. Its drooping fronds dripped the morning's raindrops as they ruffled in the breeze, but it was a nice respite from the hot July sun. The fallen pink flowers and crisp pods made up nature's comforter and she slid down dozing lightly until the annoying ping of a hammer alerted her to Nolan's return.

Her mouth was as dry as a wad of cotton. She stood and stretched lazily and walked the few yards separating them, unaware that she had had Nolan's full attention for several minutes.

"If you'll help squeeze the lemons for lemonade, I'll help you hang that door," she offered when she found him trying to balance the screen in its hinges and hammer the bolt in at the same time.

Nolan's eyes lingered on her pedicured toes before traveling up legs that seemed to go on forever, past the pale pink shorts and open-throated shirt, and finally to her dark eyes.

From smoldering blue eyes, his appreciation was blatantly obvious. Strangely her heart was racing faster now than when he had been her faceless attacker. A tingling sensation flicked up her spine, his physical male potence setting a fire inside her, an inferno she didn't believe lemonade could begin to extinguish.

"Another set of hands would help and an ice-cold drink sounds great." He positioned the screen against the side of the house and passed his hand low in front of him. "After you."

"Would you mind cutting the lemons? I want to put on some shoes and I'll be right back."

Nolan nodded and opened the refrigerator, removing the plastic bag of lemons.

After a little searching, Alinda found a pair of athletic socks and pulled them over her feet. Her heart pounded anew when she thought of the way Nolan had eyed her so thoroughly when she had stepped onto the porch. He was attracted to her. He tried to hide it, but every once in a while she noticed a certain gleam in his blue eyes. She smiled as she laced up her leather aerobic shoes. When she returned to the kitchen she wondered why such a thought should make her feel so suddenly lighthearted and carefree.

"I was hoping if I took long enough, you'd have all the lemons squeezed. It looks as if my timing was almost perfect."

He glanced at her with a smile and then turned back to

71

his chore. "I should have known. That's probably the only reason you asked me to join you." He gave the last lemon another shove against the juicer. "Done." He washed his hands and leaned against the cabinet to let Alinda finish the job.

"I must have slept longer than I thought." She took a pitcher down, to which she added water and sugar and finally the lemon juice, extracting a few seeds. "I see you've fixed the window." She filled the rest of the pitcher with ice and topped it with a few slices of lemon. While she stirred it, Nolan set two tall glasses on the cabinet next to the pitcher.

"Let's go out on the porch," Alinda suggested after she had filled the glasses.

Nolan sat down on the top step, turning sideways to lean on the wooden post. His tanned legs, naked to the fringe of his cutoffs, were stretched out in front of him. Their feet were almost touching as Alinda propped herself against the opposite post. They sat in companionable silence for a long time, stealing covert glances at each other. A hummingbird came to the feeder and stuck its beak into a hole in the plastic sunflower. Neither spoke until it flitted away.

"Did you fill the feeder with sugar water?" Alinda asked.

"Earlier, while you were sleeping." He took a long drink of his lemonade. "I thought you might enjoy it."

"Thank you. I know I will." She was touched by his thoughtfulness. No one had ever done anything like that for her without being asked; it was strange how the small gesture brought such a warm feeling. She heard the ice clink in his glass and looked in his direction. "Would you like some more?"

"I'll get it." He filled his glass and remained standing,

leaning against the rail, his legs crossed at the ankles in a deceptively relaxed pose. "Would you like to go to the Highway Nine Landing and rent a couple of jet skis tomorrow?"

Alinda chewed on her bottom lip. She wanted to get to know him, but she wondered if it was wise to cultivate a personal friendship with him. She was willing to bet he was a fugitive, but from what? The law? Cohorting thugs? Or something as simple as an ex-wife wanting her alimony? She knew she would enjoy his company, maybe a little too much, and she didn't want anything clouding her judgment if she found out he had, indeed, done something underhanded. Accepting his offer might cause him to misinterpret her feelings and that might work in her favor, or it could backfire. Was she willing to take the chance?

"You want to keep busy and it's a long time between visitors out here for me." He shrugged, as if it made little difference to him one way or the other, when in truth, every inch of his six-foot-one frame was tensed, waiting for her answer.

"It sounds tempting," she wavered. Running from imaginary fears would not get her to the truth, but spending time with Nolan Taylor just might.

"Then come with me." His smile made her decision much easier.

"All right." She agreed. "If you'll let me help around here today."

"Let's start with the screen door." He meshed the screen with the hinges then shifted his position so that Alinda could slip underneath his arm and take his place. "I need you to hold the screen steady while I tap the bolts in."

As she held it, she watched him, not with the detach-

73

ment she would have liked, though. His shirtless torso revealed the definition of his rippling muscles, covered with a fine sheen of perspiration, tanned and glistening in the late afternoon sun as he reached to tap in the top bolt. Long, lean legs bent to accommodate his bulk with ease after he tackled the middle one, wrestling to mesh the hinge just right. The working, woodsy smell of him wafted to her on a southern breeze, filling her senses with a delicious tingle. The pinging of the hammer, forcing the final bolt into place brought her back to reality.

"What next?" she asked with a forced casualness.

Nolan rummaged around in a box until he found a well-worn pair of work gloves. "Put these on. You can start by raking the leaves in several small piles."

Alinda raked water-drenched leaves and tried to restore some order to the flowerbeds while Nolan stacked the larger limbs and debris. After what seemed like hours, Alinda caught Nolan watching her under hooded lids and she wondered what he must be thinking. She pushed her wind-tangled hair from her face knowing she must look a fright. Even though physically exhausted after very little sleep the night before, then the drive to Indian Paintbrush, and the wrestling match with Nolan, Alinda was determined to prove that she could be of help. She pried her fingers from the rake and slowly moved the stiff joints. The gloves clung to her raw palms where blisters had formed. If she bent over one more time, she feared she wouldn't be able to raise up again, so it was a great relief when Nolan's deep-timbred voice echoed her own thoughts.

"It's getting dark. Let's call it a day. If the wind dies down tomorrow, we'll burn this pile and have a nice bonfire."

Alinda nodded, too tired to even speak. And when she

entered the house, she didn't want to eat either. She took a hot shower and fell into the four-poster bed, thinking nothing had ever felt so good to her, completely forgetting the dinner she had planned.

Nolan's better judgment never seemed to be able to assert itself where Alinda Sterling was concerned. Today was no exception. First he had taken her to Lake Eufaula for the afternoon and then he had accepted her dinner invitation.

His heart had soared when she, with the summer sunshine in her smile, had promised there were no ill-effects from his mistaken attack the morning before and at the same time, it was a jarring reminder of what their relationship really was. She could back out of their bargain at any time, putting him in a very precarious situation. He still had a little over four months. It was a long time to have one's life in a woman's hands.

He had decided no matter how spoiled the beautiful Alinda Sterling, he would pander to her every whim, anything it took to keep her happy. His life might very well depend on it.

Surprisingly, she turned out to be delightfully easygoing and accommodating. It was the closest he had come to an actual date in several years. He had thoroughly enjoyed her company, her wit and her intelligence an aphrodisiac any man would have had a hard time resisting. Miraculously, his hands had never strayed beyond the bounds of propriety. The sight of her in a bathing suit, its covering just enough to intrigue the imagination and inflame the senses, had made it almost impossible to keep their relationship on a platonic basis.

Her skin was slowly tanning a deliciously toasty hue and he had envied the very water that dripped from her body as she rose from the lake. It had glistened on her skin, the sun reflecting the droplets like tiny diamonds. He longed to know if she felt as wonderful as she had looked.

Nolan quickened his pace, cursing with the lengthening stride. He had to stop thinking of her as a desirable female and bear in mind at all times what a real threat she posed.

The sun was slipping closer to the horizon and he had promised Alinda that he would set the brush on fire tonight. The door to the kitchen stood open and he entered with a perfunctory knock, forcing an air of nonchalance. "Something smells great."

Alinda turned and smiled her most beguiling smile. Several times earlier in the afternoon, she had seen a certain look of longing in his eyes. If she played her cards right, she was sure it was only a matter of time before he confided in her. Yes, tonight she would get him to open up. Tonight she would charm him into telling her the story of his life and then she would have him right where she wanted and there would be no further need for a private detective. "I hope you like Southern fried chicken."

"I'd never trust a man who didn't."

"Good. I thought we could eat outside by the fire." Alinda noticed that he had changed the ever-present chambray work shirt for a knit pastel with horizontal stripes. On some men, the colors would have looked feminine, but on Nolan they accentuated his virility, his tanned skin made all the darker by the pale colors. The fabric hugged the lean contours of his chest and the rippling muscles that flattened his torso. She forced her attention to the frying chicken. Her cheeks grew warm at the remembrance of those muscles bared to her, bunching

76

and flexing as he worked. She moved around the kitchen, making last-minute preparations for the picnic and hoped Nolan would attribute the flush in her cheeks to the heat from the stove.

"I'm going to start the fire and then I'll come help you carry everything out."

"Fine. I'll only be a few more minutes." Alinda removed the chilled wine from the refrigerator and placed it on a wicker tray covered with a cotton print napkin. Then she added the hot chicken, fresh carrot and celery sticks with a delicious vegetable dip, and chunks of cantaloupe. She scanned the room, more for an extra minute to gather courage than to make sure she hadn't forgotten anything.

It was a perfect evening, Alinda thought as she stepped outside. The sky was clear and there was just enough breeze to chase away the humid heat.

Nolan took the food-laden tray while Alinda spread the blanket a safe distance from the bonfire. Flames were already licking up to the top of the huge pile. Nolan reclined on the blanket, his head propped up by his elbow, while his other hand brought a crispy drumstick to his lips. "This is delicious. I didn't realize you could cook."

"There's probably a number of things you haven't realized about me, Mr. Taylor."

He was beginning to think she was right. Yesterday she had proven her mettle by working with him all afternoon, uncomplaining, never slacking up and tonight she had cooked dinner for him. He would have never bet on either prospect. Now she sat across from him, a slight pout on her sensual lips and he knew she had no idea what a breathtakingly provocative woman she was in the firelight. He watched her lips close around a juicy piece of fruit and his imagination went wild. He focused on the fire and searched for an innocuous subject that would keep his mind off the dangerously erotic path it was trying to take. "What did you do after we got back today?"

"I promised to help with a benefit my sister is chairing. I spent a couple of hours jotting down plans for it."

"What sort of plans?"

Alinda looked at him oddly. "Would you really like to hear? I'd appreciate the chance to sound them out before I present them to the committee, but I wouldn't want to bore you."

"I'll take my chances."

She wiggled around to face him and tucked her legs beneath her, Indian style. Her face lit up and it was obvious she really enjoyed the creativity. "What do you think about an evening dedicated to the thirties, forties, and fifties? Maybe an hour or two dedicated to each era. It could be called The Big Band Bash or something like that."

Nolan thought over her proposal and answered honestly, "There would be a large amount of preparation in trying to cover three eras, different decorations, possibly different bands."

"I was hoping to find one band that could cover the whole evening with a wide range of songs. The cocktail hour could be thirties music—"

Nolan interrupted, "Waitresses could dress and carry trays in the style of cigarette girls in the thirties."

Alinda nodded. "That's a great idea. Why do I get the feeling you've done this before?"

He shrugged nonchalantly. "You inspire me."

Fishing through the raw vegetables, Alinda found the last carrot stick and dipped it in the sour cream and herb mixture. "After dinner, The Andrews Sisters' sound would be perfect, and then top the evening off with fifties music."

"Get their adrenaline pumping before you ask them to empty their pockets, right?"

"That's putting it a little crudely. It is for a good cause."

"What is this good cause? I don't believe you mentioned it."

"The Children's Hospital."

"Ah, yes. I think on the whole your idea has merit, but I think it has a few expensive holes in it. If it's charity, don't you think you should make sure all the fat's trimmed?"

"You're the most cynical man I have ever met. Are you insinuating that I would waste the donations?"

"No, I'm not saying anything of the kind. I just think you should give a thought to the final expenses before you put your plan into action."

"A whole committee will discuss my ideas before taking a final vote. Several people will have input, not just me." She had never been so sensitive to criticism. Why did Nolan Taylor's opinion count so much? He was so condescending, Alinda wanted to flounce back to the main house, but her inbred dignity won out. She remembered what this dinner was supposed to accomplish and so far, he had done all the questioning.

She leaned back, and beneath coal-dark lashes peeked over at him. In a tone she hoped sounded innocently conversational, she asked, "What did you do before you came to Indian Paintbrush?"

"A little bit of everything, and a whole lot of nothing."

So much for straightforwardness. She didn't believe him for a minute. He was too world-weary, too intense to spend his life drifting and she told him so.

He laughed uneasily, and warned, "Don't play amateur psychologist with me, Mrs. Sterling."

The tone in his voice was a little disconcerting. It brought Alinda up short. No matter how she started, he always put an abrupt halt to her probing. Why would a man close himself off so completely, unless he had something to hide?

Nolan turned the conversation around to Alinda's sister and soon had solicited a whole slew of information about her niece and nephew. They laughed together at the stories Alinda repeated about the children's antics. Their moods lightened until Nolan asked, "Did you want to have children?"

Staring into the fire, Alinda was quiet, contemplative for a long time. "We were always so complete, just the two of us," she finally answered. "Jackson and I only discussed children once, and that was after his illness was diagnosed as terminal. He regretted not having any, I know. It's so sad that we go through life with the attitude that there's always tomorrow. I found out the hard way that that isn't always true." She met Nolan's eyes and there was a void in their depths that haunted her. "How about you?"

"The opportunity never presented itself, so I've never given it any thought one way or the other."

"You've never been married?"

"No." He stood, effectively ending her inquisition. "It's late and I've got a busy day tomorrow."

Alinda gathered the remains of their meal and Nolan folded the blanket. They walked back up the hill to the main house. Alinda wanted to probe further, but there was a sadness in his eyes, a loneliness that made her stop within the imaginary bounds he had set. She was softening towards him, involving herself in a way that would be hard to pull away, no matter what the circumstances.

She took the first step up to the porch and turned to face him. Her breath caught in her throat. His lips were perilously close to hers, their eyes level.

"Thanks for dinner. It was a fine meal," he said huskily.

His breath fanned her face and Alinda thought of the old-fashioned word *swoon,* and suddenly knew exactly what it meant. "I'm glad you enjoyed it. Good night." She turned quickly and entered the house, heart pounding, suddenly afraid that winning at her own game might mean losing. She was completely, hopelessly confused.

One golden-brown eyebrow cocked over a piercing blue eye as Nolan stood, staring at the closed door. God, she was tempting! He wanted to believe she was just what she appeared to be, a breath of fresh air blown into his stale life. He shook his head. He'd lived too long, seen too much to take anything at face value, especially if it was free. He wanted to let go, though. Just once, he wanted to give in to his emotions, to love a woman to distraction. But that wasn't going to happen—not tonight, not ever.

Nolan left the shelter of the veranda and took the path to his cabin, his chin jutted low and his hands knotted in his pockets. Once inside, he stripped off his shirt and unbuckled his belt. At that point, he wandered over to the window that afforded him a full view of the main house. Whatever made him consent to this kind of life? If he had any guts at all, he would throw caution out the window and take that path right back up the hill. He jerked the pull down the teeth of the zipper in discontent and slipped out of the jeans, hopping on one foot for a moment when his foot caught and then slung them across the wooden ladder-back chair in the corner. The last

81

thing he needed was to fall in love—and with a prominent widow who had the power to destroy him. He was going off the deep end, but what a way to go, he thought as he tried to sleep, tried to go where he could safely dream of the way her lips meshed with his. With a smile on his mouth and in his heart, he fantasized without any chance of being caught. The sheets felt cold against his warm skin. It was going to be a long night.

Nolan woke with a splitting headache and a temper to match any grizzly's. He swilled down a cup of hot coffee and promptly cursed when it burned his tongue. With determined strides, he headed for the main house. His day had already started later than usual, but before he did another thing, he was going to tell Alinda, in no uncertain terms, that it was time she left Indian Paintbrush. She was a distraction he couldn't afford. Besides, he was too old for games and too good at them to ever lose to an amateur like her.

He took the first step up to the porch and froze. Alinda's voice floated through the screen. Did she have company? He took the remaining steps quietly, not intending to eavesdrop, rather, not wanting to intrude. It quickly became obvious that it was a one-sided conversation, and Nolan deduced she was on the phone. He raised his fist to knock, but her words made him draw back, and cocking his head in her direction, he couldn't believe his ears.

"No, I didn't come up here to play detective. You've found something out about him, haven't you? Otherwise, you wouldn't be making such an issue out of my being here."

There was a long pause, while Nolan listened, puzzling out what she had said.

"Maybe we should hire another detective. Nolan Taylor didn't just drop from the moon two years ago."

Nolan's fist balled at his side. The woman was having him investigated! *Damn her!* His teeth clenched together as he fought back the primal instincts of self-preservation and concentrated on the remainder of her conversation.

"Don't worry. I'll be fine, Robert. Yes, I'll call you as soon as I get back to Tulsa."

Don't worry! That was absurd. She was digging in a mine field! He had been right about her, but somehow it wasn't very comforting. Her attention was motivated by curiosity and greed rather than a genuine desire to get to know him. He stood there, his shadow cast behind him as the morning sun intensified. What should he do?

She was constantly forcing him to consider his alternatives, thrusting him into corners that made him question his every word, his every step, and he hated her for it.

He could walk away, today. Or he could take his chances, tough it out a few more months. He had covered his tracks pretty well and Baker had assured him odds were in his favor that all would be wrapped up by the end of the year. He had to be patient. Above all, he couldn't let himself be panicked into a foolish move.

He concentrated on relaxing the furrows between his brow and forced the disappointment to the back of his mind. He didn't have much room to criticize because he had been using her too. He cursed himself for underestimating her, but it wouldn't happen again.

Alinda jumped when the hard knock barely preceded Nolan's appearance behind the gray mesh screen. How long had he been standing there? She tried to think back on the conversation. Had she said anything about the investigation? Of course she had. Had she mentioned his name? She couldn't remember. She was a basket of nerves, trying desperately not to let it show.

"I see the phones are fixed." He fought hard not to let his expression betray the violence of his inner emotions.

"Yes, yes, they are," Alinda stumbled. The atmosphere was thick with his unspoken accusations. "I talked to my sister earlier, and she liked my ideas for the ball. I told her I would buy two tickets since it was for a good cause." She knew she was babbling at ninety miles a minute, but her nervous system had taken over her vocal cords. "I don't see any point in wasting the extra one. Would you like to use it?" Had she lost her mind? She could only pray he would turn her down.

As Nolan seemed to carefully mull over her invitation, she had second thoughts. Maybe asking him had not been such a bad idea. Why was it taking him so long to make a decision? Skepticism and mistrust flitted across her brow. Was he afraid to leave the secluded ranch? Was there some reason he didn't want to go to Tulsa? Or couldn't? "It's all right if you would prefer not to."

Nolan was silent for a long time, watching Alinda flutter around the room like a panicked butterfly. He needed to find out just how much she had learned from this investigation, for his own sake as well as hers, but to be seen in public was foolhardy. Yet, if he made a pretense of normality, she might call off the investigation. If she thought he was hiding from something, her interest would more than likely be piqued. Her betrayal could no longer be pushed back to some vague gray area of his brain. She had forced him to face the actuality of her deceit. It could be dangerous for everyone concerned if her detective managed to break the carefully erected barriers that had, so far, kept him alive.

When she arched an eyebrow skeptically, her chin

tilted in haughty challenge, it was the impetus he needed to accept. "No, it sounds like fun." Nolan eyed her speculatively. "I haven't danced in years. I'm not sure how good a partner I'll make."

Alinda thought briefly of his tall, hard, bronzed physique and his high cheekbones below the wide-set blue eyes and knew that once in his arms, no woman would care if he could dance! "I'll let you know the details. It's still several weeks away."

"I better get to work. Have you decided when you're going home?"

"Probably tomorrow. I need to get back for a meeting."

"Since you fixed dinner last night, tonight will be my treat." When she smiled and nodded, he went on, "My cabin. Six o'clock?"

"I'll be there. Can I bring anything?"

Nolan eyed her from head to toe, took a deep breath and said, "Just yourself."

It made Alinda extremely nervous. She wondered and speculated about that particular look all day. She worried that she was in over her head. She couldn't tease a man like Nolan Taylor and expect to walk away when the game was no longer under her control. She debated what to wear, wishing she had given more thought to wardrobe when she eyed the limited outfits that she had brought with her. She finally decided on a snug pair of white jeans and a bright yellow silk blouse splashed with white orchids. She left it loose and flowing across her breast and hips instead of tucking it in. The fabric was dressy and sensually casual at the same time. A yellow and blue cloisonné butterfly clipped back one side of her hair and a little makeup was added to enhance her casual appearance.

It was five after six when Alinda knocked on the heavy door at the front of Nolan's cabin. Her face was flushed from the brisk walk and her smile was anxious when Nolan pushed back the screen to let her in.

He watched her as she crossed the room. His eyes took in the expensive butterfly in her dark hair and his imagination flared as the silk swayed and clung to her figure in a tantalizing manner. Her jeans accentuated her delicately rounded hips and long, lean legs that ended in a teasing glimpse of her ankles and dainty feet tucked into yellow leather skimmers.

When she turned to face him, quietly questioning his silence, she was greeted by cloudy blue eyes, brooding and passionate.

Nolan cleared his throat and had to bite his tongue when he felt the overwhelming urge to suggest that they skip dinner. "It's almost ready. Would you mind setting the table while I dish everything up?"

She removed cutlery and dishes as Nolan directed her and began to set the table. They worked in synchronized precision until both stooped to retrieve a spoon Alinda had dropped. Shoulders collided and hands brushed as they both picked up the utensil and stood. Eyes clashed, hearts skyrocketed, and passion leaped between them as the light touch of his fingers on her cool skin set off sparks of desire that no caressing grasp ever could.

The kitchen suddenly seemed too small for the two of them, the setting sun emphasizing the feeling of intimacy in the dim room. His hand slipped under her large silk sleeve and curved around her upper arm, caressing the soft flesh. As if subconsciously denying his actions, he did not dip his head to hers, but instead drew her up to reach him and garnered some satisfaction from the glittering disturbance reflected in her dark eyes. There was no controlling the raw hunger that swept through him when the softness of her lips was only a breath away. His hand moved upward to knead her softly rounded shoulder and pulled her closer, pressing her breasts against his chest as his lips snared hers and their tongues intertwined.

Relaxing totally, melting into him, Alinda unconsciously dropped the stainless flatware. It clattered to the floor, jarring them both from the passionate embrace.

Nolan stepped back and stared at the offending utensil. Had she dropped it on purpose? His eyes flew to hers, but before he could read anything in their huge round depths, he smelled searing meat and moved quickly to turn out all the flames. Luckily the food was all salvageable.

Unknowingly, Nolan revealed a lot to Alinda when he served her. It wasn't a meat and potatoes meal. It was butterfly pork chops sautéed in a delicate sauce, fresh steamed asparagus drizzled with butter and an attractively arranged fruit plate. They were dishes she might serve at an elaborate dinner party. "Did you do this yourself?" she asked, wanting to return their relationship to a polite, casual level after the kiss they had shared only moments ago.

"Yes. I got a late start this morning and I had to improvise on dinner."

"It would have taken me hours to put this together," she said incredulously.

"No, it's simple. It took me thirty minutes, forty, tops."

"Mmmm, very delicious. Where did you learn to cook?"

Nolan hesitated. "My mother. She had a restaurant when I was very young."

"Oh, really. Where?"

Nolan stood. "I forgot the wine." He was tempted to

take a long swallow from the bottle, but instead, he poured it in two tumblers. "No wineglasses," he said in a dry, caustic tone. "It shouldn't affect the taste, only the atmosphere."

Unwilling to be distracted by his cynicism when she was on the verge of learning something about this mystery man, Alinda asked, "Where did you say your mother was from?"

"I didn't." Nolan chewed a bite of the tender pork, wondering how he was going to get out of this. Should he lie? A good detective could take the truth and run with it. He glanced at Alinda and she was showing no signs of dropping the subject. "California," he lied. Something in his gut wrenched. He was used to lying. But lying to Alinda left a bad taste in his mouth.

"Where in California?"

"Los Angeles." With no hesitation, he lied again. At least if a detective checked out his story, it would take weeks to discover he had sent him on a wild goose chase. Pondering on the deceptive casualness of her questions the last few days, and the heart-wrenching scene in Robert's office, he concluded she was a very good actress. Almost good enough to make him want to believe her. *Stop right there, Taylor.* He was crossing very dangerous ground.

"What was the name of it? I've been there several times."

"I was very young." His chair leg scraped impatiently against the tiled floor as he pushed back from the table. Standing, he moved to the counter where he had left the wine bottle and filled his glass. "I don't really remember what the name was. Have you given any more thought to the ball?" he asked as he tipped the bottle to refill her glass also.

Alinda got the message. She backed off, for now. She didn't want it to appear obvious that she was pumping him for information. If she persisted in questioning him, he might catch on.

"As a matter of fact, I thought we might print up tickets to look like old-fashioned dance cards and the ladies sell their dances. If you want to dance with the lady, you have to make a donation."

"Clever idea."

Alinda pretended mock surprise. "You mean you like it?"

"I like it."

After dinner, they shared the kitchen chores and discussed the date and time of the ball. Nolan insisted on escorting Alinda back to the main house even after she argued that it wasn't necessary. Nolan was adamant. Alinda's curiosity was aroused once again. It wasn't that far. Was he just being a gentleman or was there more to it?

In the faint glow of the porch light, Nolan found it hard to believe this woman's motives were greed. She had an ethereal beauty that he found hard to resist, an open smile that beckoned.

Suddenly, he frowned and tilted his head, listening intently.

"What is it?" she asked, not hearing anything unusual.

"Shhh."

Then she heard. "It's only a car."

Nolan's frown deepened as the hum of an engine grew closer. "Stay here. I'm going to walk around front."

"I'm not staying on this porch by myself."

Against his better judgment, he grabbed her hand roughly and pulled her along behind him. "All right, but stay behind me and shut up."

They stood in the shadows of the north side of the house, waiting. For what, Alinda had no idea. Her breathing was deep, but short. Nolan's was so even she could hardly tell he was breathing at all.

The truck drove on by and Nolan's shoulders visibly relaxed. "It was Cy. He must have had a rodeo tonight."

Even in the dark, he could see the burning curiosity in her eyes. It was becoming harder and harder to come up with plausible excuses for his actions. "We live a long way from any law enforcement. There aren't many people that have any business out this far. I just like to keep an eye on who's coming and going." He could tell it wasn't enough to completely satisfy her inquisitive nature. He decided to change the subject, hoping to keep her from dwelling on his motives. "You're leaving in the morning?"

"Yes." Her voice was a whisper, carried away by the night breeze. She shivered as he ran a finger up her silk-clad arm.

Passion leaped into his eyes and his hand curved sensuously around her neck. His head dipped toward her, blocking out the moon and the stars, everything but the feel of his lips tenderly laced with hers. She never wanted his hard male lips to stop their unchaste assault. But she knew she had to put an end to it. Their relationship could not move from wary adversaries to . . . to anything. She gently pushed against his chest and ducked her head. "I've enjoyed my stay. I'll see you for the ball in a few weeks."

Nolan nodded, angry with himself for not being able to resist her. Five minutes too late, he forced himself to remember that this devious woman was trying to uncover something he had spent years hiding—something his life depended on keeping concealed. She wasn't the innocent that she appeared to be. Above all, he had to keep that in mind. The woman that his body ached to hold, a woman that was kind and sweet and friendly, in reality did not exist. With that thought, he was able to turn away, but not without glancing back, not without wishing things were different.

Alinda entered the house and considered whether Jackson would have approved of what she was doing. An inner voice told her that Nolan Taylor wasn't capable of what she had accused him of in Robert's office, but the mystery surrounding him gnawed at her. If he was on the up and up, why was his life such a secret? Why didn't he level with her?

She went to bed, plagued by questions. Was her curiosity overshadowed by her better judgment? He was definitely an intriguing man, but that was as far as it went, she told herself, pounding the lumps out of the hard pillow.

CHAPTER SIX

Alinda paced the foyer. *Honestly,* she chastised herself. *You'd think I was going on a real date.* She had talked to Nolan only once since her visit to the ranch and that was to tell him that the committee had decided to require dress in the style of one of the three eras.

The chimes rang and her pacing ended. Nervously, she tugged at the hem of her shoulder-padded jacket and smoothed the matching straight skirt.

"Would you like me to answer it?" Mary asked.

"No, I'll get it," she answered, opening one side of the stained-glass door, her heart pounding furiously in her chest.

He looked incredibly handsome, a cross between Humphrey Bogart and Al Capone, devilishly daring, wickedly unrepentant in the double-breasted suit and baggy trousers, his hat sitting low over one eye, cloaking his expression in mystery. And when he took his hat off, turning the brim between his lean fingers, looking shyly romantic, he was a delicious mixture of Paul Newman and Robert

Redford. She thought, ironically, his costume was very fitting. In real life, he seemed at odds also.

"May I come in?" His voice was low and challenging, a tightness around his mouth that was becoming all too familiar.

"Of course, I'm sorry." Alinda sensed his uneasiness and wondered if it was due to their arrangement or the fact that he would be faced with her friends for an entire evening.

Nolan stared at the obvious wealth and taste that went into decorating Alinda's home. He had almost forgotten people still live this way, tucked away in the safe haven of wealth. He turned his attention to Alinda. She looked so prim in her fitted suit, buttoned from her small neck to her trim waist, and her hair rolled around her face in a tight coiffure. He wondered if she had deliberately chosen the outfit to discourage any advances he might be tempted to make. Little did she know, in his eyes she couldn't have been more provocative dressed in red satin and fishnet stockings. Unfortunately, the crisp, elegant look only tempted him into trying to persuade her to shed the carefully controlled image. His gaze devoured her, yet his body tensed as he fought to resist the urge to let his emotions take free rein. He couldn't forget why he had accepted her invitation. He couldn't trust her, not for even one night.

He inquired, "Are you ready?"

His voice was deep and held a trace of challenge. There was something in his manner that bothered her. She had decided that he had not overheard her conversation with Robert, but his attitude tonight seemed so different. It was a little unnerving. Alinda frantically tried to come up with a plausible excuse not to go. The crowd would be in a buzz over her newfound escort. Was it too soon after

Jackson's death to appear in public with a man? It was ludicrous to let her involvement with him become common knowledge. When the real truth about him was out, she might never live it down.

But since when did she care what other people thought? she chided herself. Putting the ridiculous ideas down to last-minute jitters was the most sensible thing she had done in the last half hour. She picked up her handbag and knew it was too late for regrets as she suggested they take her car. She was doing this for Jackson. She could survive a little tongue wagging if it brought her closer to the truth.

"Your tie is crooked." Reaching across the seat to straighten it before Nolan started the engine, her fingers lingered on the knot a little longer than was necessary. She looked at him and saw an expression on his face that she had never seen before. "You're enjoying this?" she questioned, a surprised smile in her eyes.

He caught her hand when she started to move away and brought it to his lips. "It's been a long time since I was fussed over by a lovely lady."

"That must mean there was someone special in your life at some point."

"My mother," he revealed with an infuriatingly charming grin on his face. He put the Mercedes in gear and followed the circular drive onto Yorktown. Nothing gave away his inner turmoil, his anxiousness at being surrounded by a crowd after four years of seclusion, or his fear of being recognized.

She didn't miss a chance to dig, he thought. He was going to have to be very careful tonight. The most innocent comment seemed to trigger her curiosity.

He left the car with the valet and took a deep cleansing breath as he walked around the rear of the polished automobile. It did not calm the racing of his heart as he went through the motions of playing the attentive escort.

Their entrance at the club drew a number of stares and dropped chins. Alinda's hand shook slightly on Nolan's arm and he covered it with his in an unconsciously reassuring gesture as his eyes darted around the opulent room, quickly making note of the fire exits and the door that he assumed led to the kitchen.

"Alinda," Jan called and waved from a crowd of committee members.

The pulse in Nolan's temple began to throb with unerring consistency. But his hesitation was only momentary before he let Alinda lead the way toward the waving group, stopping several times to greet friends and curious acquaintances, making brief introductions before politely moving on. She introduced Nolan to everyone, saving her sister for last.

After a proper hello, Jan leaned over to whisper, "No wonder you've kept him hidden at the ranch, Alinda. It's positively sinful for anyone to be that handsome."

A couple was elaborating on the cruise they had recently taken and Nolan eyed Jan as she smiled mischievously and whispered in Alinda's ear.

There were obvious similarities and differences in the sisters, but Nolan had never seen such a teasing sparkle in Alinda's eyes, that zest for life that Jan displayed. He took the brief respite from Alinda's curious appraisal to survey the room once again.

Deep in thought, Nolan was caught completely off guard when a young photographer snapped the group's picture. His eyes narrowed and he cursed under his breath, turning away quickly as the photographer took several more. Anxiety tore at his gut. He pasted a false smile on his face and asked Alinda, "Who the hell is that?"

"The committee hired him to take pictures to sell to the guests and some publicity photos for tomorrow morning's *Daily News.*"

Nolan watched the photographer move around the room with sharply narrowed eyes and wondered how in blazes he was going to contend with this new problem. Unaware that he had circled Alinda's wrist in a punishing grip, he demanded, "Was this your idea, also?"

"Yes, it was. Why?" she questioned before fiercely whispering, "You're hurting me."

He relaxed his hold and easily slipped his hand into hers, ignoring her question.

The atmosphere was suddenly riddled with tension and Alinda rushed to explain, although she wasn't sure why. "It'll be a great way to bring in more money. We're paying him ten percent of every photo sold. The rest will go to charity."

Nolan smiled wryly and pretended to concentrate on the conversation as it centered on the dance cards. He had to get at that film and get out of here. *Whoa, Taylor. Don't panic.* If he left this early, more eyebrows might be raised, thus drawing even more attention. He could ride it out. By the end of the evening, he could come up with a way to handle the photographer.

The rigidity of his body extended to the hand that clasped Alinda's and she eyed him with apprehension. He seemed ready to spring at the slightest movement. At that moment, she would have given anything to know what was going on in his mind. She feared him and at the same time feared for him.

Jan's husband, Mike, interrupted her introspection by insisting on being the first to sign Alinda's dance card.

Nolan's arm circled her waist in a strangely possessive way, and he stood quietly while Mike signed the first line. But when another man started to ask for a dance, Nolan took the card and signed the rest of the spaces.

Alinda tried to stop him. "Nolan, you can't do that. Please," she whispered, discreetly tugging at his sleeve. "You're embarrassing me."

He handed her the card, and turned to the man that stood with his mouth open. "As you can see, the lady is booked solid."

The man laughed uneasily, nodded and turned away.

"I hope you know you just signed for over two hundred dollars' worth of donations."

"You're worth every penny."

Jan leaned over to whisper, "And charming too, you lucky devil."

"Would you like a drink?" Nolan asked, unperturbed by Alinda's deadly glare.

"Something strong. I have a feeling I'm going to need it," she commented dryly.

They had time for only one drink before dinner was announced. Nolan held Alinda's chair, then seated himself and spread his napkin across his thighs when the spinach salad was served.

Alinda's attention was drawn by the contrast between the tanned strength of his hands and the white linen napkin he shook over his lap. She wondered what those hands could do in the heat of passion, how they would feel against her bare skin . . .

"Alinda, don't you agree?"

"Yes, yes, I do." She glanced at Nolan and the slight upward tilt of his lips told her he knew she had no idea what she was agreeing with.

During the first course, Nolan was strangely quiet, but

as the meal progressed, he seemed to relax, knowledgeably discussing a variety of subjects. Alinda was a little surprised at how well he fit in as she listened to him comment on a new solar theory. When he was asked what he did for a living, he simply said, "I run a ranch."

She had to bite her tongue to keep from spitefully clarifying his statement. The tightness around Nolan's mouth and the intense direction of his gaze dared her to do it. She couldn't ever remember feeling so ill at ease. The way he looked at her made her want to squirm in her seat.

Dirty dishes were cleared away and coffee served before the music for the first dance was played. Mike came to escort Alinda to the dance floor. He held her in a loose embrace and smiled at her pensive expression. "Is dancing with your brother-in-law so distasteful?"

"No, of course not." She shook her head and smiled.

"You're really very lucky, you know."

"How's that?" she asked warily.

"To have someone so interested in you that he would pay two hundred and twenty-five dollars just for the privilege of dancing with you."

"Is that how you see it?"

"That's how I see it. After all, I only signed one of Jan's lines."

"That's because you used some propriety in your judgment," Alinda said.

Nolan wasted no time in claiming her for the second dance. There was a flurry of activity around the dance floor. "This was a good idea. It's much more exciting than your run-of-the-mill fund raiser."

Alinda thanked him for his compliment, wondering how many other fund raisers he had attended.

"Are you angry because by signing your card, I kept you from dancing with someone else? Maybe a married

98

man that could have used this as a ruse to hold you in his arms in front of everyone and not be condemned for it?" he taunted with quiet savagery. A wary anger glinted in his eyes, but it was quickly masked.

"Don't be absurd!" She struggled to end the dance, but Nolan's strong hands held her against him. "There is no one else," Alinda answered hotly.

"Ah, the words that every man wants to hear," he countered with derision, but Alinda didn't catch the mockery in his tone.

"There is no one else except Jackson. Certainly you didn't think I was referring to you, Mr. Taylor." She emphasized the formality of his name, hoping to put some distance between them with her tart words since he seemed to be putting less between their bodies, his hold increasingly tight.

He didn't know why he was pushing her to anger, or why it was important to prove who was the stronger, physically. But somehow, allowing her to win the minor struggle was tied to winning it all so he held fast until she gave in to him.

After several more dances, Alinda's body ached from the muscles that tensed every time Nolan took her in his arms. It was a great relief to her when he suggested they take a break. Alinda declined his offer of a drink and made her way to the ladies' room. She found Jan seated on a velvet-cushioned bench in front of the mirror.

Alone, Jan used the opportunity to inquire about her sister's friend. "Now I know why you were in such a flap to get to the ranch after the storm."

"What's that supposed to mean?"

"It's supposed to mean that he's a very nice man and I can see why you're interested in him." Jan put on an

99

attractive shade of pink lipstick before glancing at Alinda.

"I'm not interested in him romantically. He doesn't do a thing for me. I simply went to the ranch to see if I could help. Period." She didn't dare reveal the real reason she had spent so much time with Nolan Taylor. She would be on the receiving end of a lecture from Jan that the likes of no Mother Superior had ever given, with putting her life in unnecessary danger being at the top of the list.

"Alinda, Jackson is the one who died, not you."

Alinda felt hurt mixed with anger, and tears sprang to her eyes. If only Jackson were here, she wouldn't feel so much as if she were beating her head against a brick wall.

"I know it's a cruel thing to say, but it's the truth. You're a young woman with a woman's needs. They won't disappear, no matter how vehemently you deny them to me, or to yourself, or to Nolan Taylor."

"You never were one for beating around the bush, were you, Jan?" Alinda dabbed at the tears and blew her nose.

Jan's voice grew soft with understanding. "It's been well over a year since Jackson became too ill to be a husband to you and months since he passed away. You have to accept it and let him go."

"I'm trying." She sniffed and wiped her eyes again.

"I know, and coming with Nolan tonight was a big step." Jan patted her sister's hand. "Speaking of which, he probably thinks you've run off. We'd better join the others."

Nolan stopped his pacing outside the ladies' room entrance as soon as Alinda appeared; his relief was acute. He searched her eyes, noting the moistness that lingered on her spiky lashes. "Are you all right?" he asked, an unguarded tenderness springing into his blue eyes.

"I'm fine." Alinda was deeply touched by his genuine

concern, especially since he was looking at her with enough charm to melt an ice cube. She wished it was all as simple as Jan had made it sound.

The band had started playing rock music and Nolan smiled down at Alinda mischievously, "Do you jitterbug?"

She nodded, but admitted, "I'm not very good."

"Then we'll be a matched pair. Care to try it with me?"

Slowly, her inhibitions slid away and Alinda relaxed. They laughed at each other's mistakes and quickly realized that the fun was in the trying. After three exhausting dances, they collapsed in each other's arms in a fit of laughter. For a while, he had helped her forget the sadness of having lost a husband and she had helped him forget there was a very real danger out there somewhere, waiting for him to make a false move.

The music changed to a slow love ballad by Elvis Presley. Nolan slipped an arm around Alinda's waist when she started to leave the dance floor, and his other hand cupped the back of her head when she started to protest. He bent down to whisper in her ear, unaware of the tiny bumps that raised up on her neck when his warm breath traveled the sensitive nerves of her ear. "Don't pull away, Ali. I've been waiting all evening for this very moment— the chance to hold you without—without . . . anything between us." *Without Jackson between us. Without Martinelli.* He wanted to tell her this, and more. He wanted to tell her how happy she made him when she laughed, and how wonderful she felt in his arms, and that if it all ended tomorrow, knowing her had made his whole life worthwhile. But, he couldn't tell her those things. Now wasn't the time. Not for her and certainly not for him.

She relaxed in his arms and reveled in the feel of his

hard body against the soft curves of her own, closed her eyes and forgot they weren't alone, forgot she would be the talk of the club tomorrow for this blatant defiance of convention. Suddenly none of it mattered except the rightness she felt in this man's arms.

When the music stopped, Alinda admitted she was ready to call it a night. "I'm exhausted."

"You're ready to leave?" He hadn't counted on her wanting to go home so early. He had to think of a way to stall her, and fast. He felt like Cinderella at the ball, with the clock ticking, perilously approaching midnight. When Mike stopped them on the way to the coat-check counter to pick up Alinda's evening bag, Nolan breathed a sigh of relief.

"You can't leave yet," Mike insisted. "I want to make a toast."

"One drink?" Alinda asked with a questioning lift of her brow.

Nolan nodded and took two glasses of wine from a passing waiter. He made a pretense at holding his glass up in a toast, but he didn't hear Mike's words of praise. His eyes narrowed shrewdly on the photographer who moved around the small group snapping pictures indiscriminately. His teeth clenched in morose displeasure and the pulse in his temple picked up its drumbeat of threatening doom. The grip he had on the wineglass tightened and with only a little more pressure, he could have splintered it into a thousand tiny pieces.

When the young man stooped behind Nolan for a better shot, Nolan took advantage of the opportunity, turned and bumped into him, knocking the photographer off balance. The camera fell to the floor and Nolan, apologizing profusely, helped the man to his feet and bent down to retrieve the camera. The group had quieted and Alinda moved to see if she could help.

Standing with a deceptively genuine look of despair on his face, Nolan apologized again in a very convincing manner. "I'm so sorry. It looks like your camera back came open." He held out the exposed film. "I don't know what to say. A whole evening's work ruined. I'll write you out a check. Just tell me how much."

For all the world, Nolan appeared genuinely contrite, but Alinda wasn't fooled. She searched the group of faces, frantic that someone had witnessed what she had. If she hadn't moved when she did, she would have been fooled also. Nolan had deliberately exposed film that could have made the Children's Hospital a lot of money. Why?

Conscious of a pair of suspicious brown eyes, Nolan faced Alinda. "Are we ready to go now?"

She only nodded to him, her mouth tight-lipped. When she turned to the group to say good night, it took enormous willpower to soften her grim expression into a smile.

Once outside, she rounded on him, "Are you crazy?"

"Sometimes I think so, yes," he admitted in a coldly amused tone of voice while loosening his tie with a jerk, then unfastening the collar button of his starched shirt.

"You deliberately exposed that film. I want to know why!"

The haughty demand only served to enrage his already seething temper. Who did she think she was demanding answers from him? She was the reason he was here in this precarious position to begin with. If not for her infernal snooping . . .

Nolan glanced around to make sure no one had overheard, then he opened the passenger door and motioned for Alinda to get in the car with a jerk of his head.

"I'm not going anywhere with you, not until you tell me why."

His eyes took on a strange quality. For a moment Alinda thought they actually glowed in the phosphorescent street lighting. It was disturbing and frightening, yet she wanted to beg him to trust her, rather than run from him. She forced the corners of her mouth to relax. Bullying him would get her nowhere. If pushed into a corner, he was the type to bite, not back down. She decided on another tactic. "You caused quite a stir."

Nolan eyed her suspiciously as she silently rescinded her threat and slid into the automobile. When he joined her in the plush interior, she faced him, her composure the antithesis to the adrenaline still coursing through him. "If you would only tell me, maybe I could help."

"I don't need anyone's help. I don't like to have my picture taken. It's as simple as that."

"Is it?" she questioned, unable to control her anger momentarily. Part of her was fed up with his half truths and deliberate vagueness, yet another part of her, a very feminine part of her, wanted to reach out and erase the torment that she saw in his eyes. And it was the latter part that drew Alinda to him this night.

"Let's go home. I'll pour you a brandy," she suggested.

"Sure you wouldn't rather I called a cab?"

"Positive."

The drive to Alinda's home was made in silence. She wanted to ask a dozen questions, but she knew he needed some breathing room and she gave it to him until she handed him the promised glass of brandy in her living room. Her eyes searched his face. What started out as casual intrigue with a strange man had turned into a genuine affection and a soul-stirring sexual awareness of Nolan Taylor.

He drank half the brandy down in one fiery gulp, coughing slightly as it burned his throat. "I'm sorry if I embarrassed you in front of your friends." He swallowed the remaining alcohol and set the crystal on the fireplace mantel.

Setting her unfinished glass next to his, Alinda faced him. "Please tell me what you're running from. Maybe I could help. I'm a very wealthy woman."

"How many times do I have to tell you I'm not one of your charities?" He laughed, a mirthless noise in his chest. "Besides, all the money in the world couldn't change my life. What's done is done."

The cliché sounded all the more fatal from the tortured expression on his face. She thought she had never seen such a sad, resigned epitaph on one's fate. It made her want to move heaven and earth to help him, to comfort him. She wanted to take him in her arms and erase all the tension so vividly outlined in his every muscle. "Nolan?" All of her feelings were transmitted with the one word. There was nothing more she could say. She had asked— no, *begged* him to let her help, and he had refused.

He grabbed her chin and watched her face, trying to discern the truth from the nuances of her expression. "Say it again," he ordered in a thick-threaded voice. "Say my name again."

"Nolan," she whispered, standing on tiptoe, entwining her arms around his neck, eliminating the shaft of light between them. "Nolan," she repeated over and over.

Her sensuous utterance of his name breached his tenuous defenses, so carefully erected and fiercely protected until now. His arms went around her waist, crushing her luscious curves against his work-hardened body. He felt a dam burst inside him; all the physical and emotional desire pent up in him was rushing over the top, flowing out of control. His lips sought hers, searching for that blissful feeling he had known with her at the pond, a feeling he had never known existed until then and had craved ever since. His mouth moved against her lips, taking charge, his tongue exploring her silky warm depths. His lean, strong hand caressed her spine, drawing her closer. He couldn't breathe, yet he didn't want to if it meant letting her go. His hands wrapped around her waist, crossing over her back and meeting under the swell of her breasts, deepening the kiss, fanning the flaming fires of his desire every time his questing tongue met with hers.

Alinda ran her fingers up and down his back, feeling his muscles bunch and relax while his hands moved over her clothed body, running impatiently over the fullness of a breast, exploring her tiny waist, and the shapely outsweep of her hips. He slid a hand under her jacket and tugged the silk chemise free from her skirt's confining waistband. His hands were warm and cool at the same time, moving against her bare skin with a fervor that ignited her senses and set her whole body on fire. When his thumbs met the hard tip of her breasts, she arched toward him seeking a satisfaction that only their two bodies melded together could produce.

Her nails tripped over his shirt buttons, loosening them so her fingers could waltz through the matted hair on his chest, her hand pausing on the wild beat of his heart, her lips following the sensual trail. "Oh, Nolan," she whispered, meeting his lips once again. Her hands danced over his shoulders and down the muscles on either side of his spine, at first a languorous ballet, then speeding up the tempo to an exotic flamenco. Her lips alternately teased and loved with a demanding pressure.

Nolan groaned deep in his chest and Alinda tilted her head back, her ardent expression meeting with his amorous blue eyes, eyes that mirrored her own longings, feelings that had been denied too long for both of them. But there was something else there too. Was it anger?

Was he giving in to the enemy? he wondered. There was a sudden brittle tension in the air as he brought his ardent emotions under control. Eyeing, with disdain, her fingers as they foraged through the matting of hair on his chest, he was reminded that this was the woman that, more than likely, had detectives leading Martinelli to his door and he was playing right into her hands.

Cursing at himself for still wanting to drop another lingering kiss on the swelling softness of her lips, he snatched Alinda's hands from his chest, ending their quest of his fevered skin, and held them still at his sides.

His body shook with his need for her and he forced himself to step away before he lost control entirely. He had never met a woman that could do more than scratch the surface of his emotions, yet this one had brazenly carved her initials in his soul. His mouth tightened grimly. He picked up her brandy snifter and tossed the remaining amber liquid down his throat. It calmed the erratic beating of his pulse and slowed his breathing, but it didn't take away the burning desire he felt for the woman still standing beside him, watching him, her expression unveiled, openly wanting him.

A multitude of emotions were going through Alinda's mind as she watched Nolan withdraw. Was she so wrapped up in her own ecstasy that she had failed to notice that the feeling wasn't mutual? Had he trembled with desire—or revulsion and contempt? Was she too naïve to know the difference? She turned from him, self-consciously straightening her clothing, deep down knowing her doubts were not rational. How did she get so carried away?

Nolan's thoughts were equally turbulent. How could he love and hate her at the same time? He had a right to be angry at her; he *was* angry at her. But, mad as he was, he couldn't bear their distance, or the sight of her stiff, proud shoulders as she turned away from him. He pulled her back against his chest, his strong hands gripping her when she tried to twist away. "Turn around and look at me, Ali."

She halfheartedly resisted, then let him turn her in his arms.

"Look at me." He shook her gently. "Please." Her confused expression made him want to run. He was in too deep. "I know you don't understand. I have no business doing this to you. It's not that I don't want you. Every part of my body is screaming for you. I just can't."

"Can't or won't?"

His hands dropped away from her, riled that he had given in to the need to comfort her. "Both," he said.

Her hands gripped his biceps, strong under the soft tips of her fingers, forcing him to give her his full attention. "Tell me. Tell me what it is," she begged.

He shook his head and turned away, breaking the fragile contact.

"You don't have to be so cavalier," she burst out angrily.

Then he smiled in a cold, amused way that sent a shiver down her spine.

"You're gorgeous when you're angry. Your face turns the most desirable shade of pink and your pupils get a spark of light in them."

"That's right," she started sarcastically. "If I hit a nerve, get flippant. Isn't that the way you operate?"

"It's the truth." A muscle at the corner of his mouth twitched. It was all true. She *was* gorgeous and he *did* resort to teasing when she got too close. It was a reflex action, the only way he knew to survive.

With an air of impatience, he slung his double-breasted jacket over his shoulder and left her with a terse, "Good-bye, Ali."

"Oh!" If she had been the violent type, she would have thrown something at his retreating back. *What was he hiding?* Why had he suddenly put an end to their loving, a deep-seated anger burning in his eyes? He must have overheard her conversation with Robert. Why else would he look at her with such contempt?

As she took the carpeted stairway to her room, his "Good-bye, Ali" echoed over and over. It sounded so final. Well, if he thought he had seen the last of her, he was sadly mistaken. She wasn't ready to give up yet.

CHAPTER SEVEN

The *Daily News* ran a very complimentary article on the Children's Hospital Benefit Ball in Sunday's society section, with a picture of several committee members and their escorts. To the newspaper's credit, it was a very good likeness of them all.

What would Nolan think when he saw it? The roll of film he had destroyed obviously wasn't the only one. No wonder the photographer hadn't seemed too perturbed, Alinda thought as she stared at Nolan's picture. He was smiling an enigmatic smile that was riddled with intrigue and charm, and it drew her thoughts back to him again and again.

After the success of the benefit dance, it didn't take long for Alinda's phone to begin ringing again with requests for help on various fund-raising committees, and even a few social engagements. The compliments and the requests were endless. As the late summer's temperatures soared well over a hundred degrees, Alinda's calendar was filled with more events than any one person could possibly attend. She had less and less time to lounge by the pool.

This schedule suited her just fine. The busier she stayed, the less time she had to dwell on Nolan Taylor. She worked like a horse from the early morning until late at night, tiring herself mentally and physically until she could fall into bed without a thought to her personal unhappiness. But no matter how busy she stayed, there was still something missing. It gnawed at her constantly and the loneliness was a growing void inside of her.

Even though she still missed Jackson, her memories of him were not as frequent and they were less painful when they did occur. Life was going on and she was being carried along in its wake. The restlessness that gripped her was another matter, she thought as she sat at her vanity removing her makeup. She released her hair from its tight knot on top of her head and brushed it vigorously.

The ballet tonight had been particularly enjoyable. She had managed to forget, for a few hours, the conversation she and Jan had had that afternoon about Nolan.

"Something happened after the ball and don't try to deny it," Jan had accused. "I could see it in your eyes last week when we had lunch at the club."

"I don't know what you mean."

"It's me, Jan, your sister. Remember? You never were good at hiding your feelings, certainly not from me. Did he make a pass at you?"

She couldn't help but smile. Pass was such an inappropriate word for what had happened between herself and Nolan. Alinda couldn't lie with her sister's stare perceiving her deepest feelings, but she could leave out a few of the details. "He kissed me."

"That's all? Did you kiss him back?" Jan had regretted

her bluntness when the tortured look entered her sister's eyes. "Oh, honey." She had put her arm around Alinda's shoulders. "Is that what's bothering you? That you responded?"

Alinda couldn't begin to explain completely so she had let Jan draw her own conclusions.

Jan had guided Alinda toward a chair and sat down to face her. "Listen to me. You're barely thirty years old. It's only natural that another man's touch would be appealing to you."

Alinda buried her face in her hands, the memory of Nolan's lips descending towards hers, his hands moving with sensual accuracy along her spine, quite vivid in her mind. "It's too soon. Besides, it would never work."

"Too soon! In that sense, it has been more than a year since Jackson was a husband to you."

"You don't understand."

Jan had tugged at her sister's hand, urging Alinda to look at her. "You of all people know how short life can be, Alinda. If you're attracted to this man, do something about it."

"I don't know," Alinda said wearily. "It's just not that simple."

It wasn't as easy as Jan had made it sound. She might be attracted to Nolan physically, but she didn't completely trust him; even Robert was beginning to believe something suspicious was going on. All the facts pointed to it—his immediate suspiciousness when he had found her in his cabin, his violent attack on her in the ranch kitchen, his angry reaction to the photographer at the ball. And whatever the explanations were for these actions, she wasn't sure she wanted to hear them.

"Let go, Alinda. Time will close yesterday's doors, if you'll only let it." Jan had poetically prophesied and when there was still indecision in Alinda's expression, she had added, "Promise me you'll think about it."

Alinda *had* given it thought—all afternoon. In fact, much of her time today had been spent wrestling with her feelings. If she went to the ranch one more time . . .

As Alinda took the familiar two-lane highway, she smiled at her own impetuousness. Jackson had always discouraged her spontaneity. The last few months, spontaneous had been her middle name.

She drove through the small town of Porter and remembered the sweet smell of ripening peaches when she had driven to Indian Paintbrush alone for the first time last spring. It seemed an eternity ago rather than only three months. The miles seemed to shed away, the scenery unfolding before her and then as quickly passing in a blur as the blacktop cut through the fields with never-ending precision.

This time she remembered her key and called out before entering the house, and after passing the threshold. She breathed a sigh, a mixture of disappointment and relief when there was no answer. She closed her eyes tightly and forced a deep breath when she recalled the finality in Nolan's tone when he had said good-bye. Now was not the time to get cold feet.

She carried in her overnight bag and the groceries she had brought. After settling in, she stepped outside and inhaled the sweet pine-scented air. Hay bales dotted the hillside. Wondering where Nolan could be, she walked over to lean idly on the porch column.

Nolan led his horse from the barn, ready for a relaxing ride after a hard day's work. He caught a flash of red and black toward the main house and turned, instantly alert. He stopped abruptly, the horse nudging his shoulder because of the unexpected halt. "What the . . ." He couldn't take his eyes off the statuesque beauty watching him. He took in every detail, from the ribbon tied around her ponytail—a style only she could carry off looking sensual rather than youthful—down to the black shorts that left her beautiful legs open to his perusal.

He looped the reins around the fence post, cursing his heart for beating faster and forced himself to slow down when he realized his pace had quickened.

What was she doing here? Had she come to cook another chicken dinner, to ply him with questions, or something much harder to resist—herself? It had almost worked before. He couldn't afford to give in this time.

His jaw tightened and he wondered for the hundredth time if she was still having him investigated. What if she was here to tell him she had discovered everything? No, that was impossible. *Calm down, Taylor.* There's no way for her to get to the truth—or so he hoped.

So why didn't he just confront her, be as honest as he could? He might be able to persuade her to drop the investigation; then again, he might just pique her interest even more. It was a risk he couldn't take. He didn't dare trust her with the truth. He couldn't trust anyone.

He remembered the article in the *Daily News* the Sunday after the ball. Normally, he didn't even read the society section, but this Sunday, he had made it a point and his worst fears had been justified. There he was in black and white. That familiar beat of impending doom drummed in his temple. His stomach churned with anger and indecision. One day he was packing and the next he was telling himself to calm down and take it one step at a time. It wasn't that long before the agreed-upon six months would be up. If he could just hold out a little longer . . .

At least they hadn't mentioned his name, only that he was the escort of Mrs. Alinda Sterling. He should have been grateful for that, but it grated on his nerves. Her escort, indeed. It had sounded as if he had paid for the privilege.

In a moment of sentimental weakness, he had torn it out and shoved it in his desk drawer and returned to look at it several times since, telling himself it was to remind him of what giving in to her had cost him, to remind him of his foolishness. It was because of this very woman that he had been suddenly exposed to thousands of readers. A picture in a widely circulated newspaper could be his undoing. Would Martinelli's tentacles reach a newspaper in the heart of the Bible Belt?

When he reached her, he had every intention of telling her to leave. Now. Today. But when he approached her, she looked so tentatively shy and unsure, he couldn't spurn her away with angry words. Totally against his better judgment, he took her in his arms and silently communicated how much he had missed her.

That day set a precedent for days to come. They rode together every afternoon except when Alinda had to return to Tulsa; then they shared long telephone conversations. He never offered to accompany her home or suggested he visit her in Tulsa. He even eliminated the short trips into the local town. If he needed something, he sent one of the hands and the housekeeper bought his groceries. After the picture in the paper, it was imperative that he lay low for a while.

During this time, Nolan struggled with his conscience. Before she came into his life, all his days ran together, a sameness about them that he never let himself dwell upon. Now that he had confined himself to the ranch, her visits meant even more. He knew he was falling in love with Alinda and he also realized that she was probably still having him investigated. He cursed himself for a fool many times, even as he let their relationship develop normally, as if it could come to a normal conclusion. Eventually he knew reality would come between them, but for now he was content to live in this fool's paradise.

One afternoon, they rode along the south boundary fence. Alinda's lighthearted banter chased away Nolan's misgivings, as it always did. She had an incredible way of making him feel they were the only two people on earth. She never brought up his past or eluded to any subjects he would have considered taboo.

"Do you think Jezebel's calf would have wandered this far?" Alinda asked.

"No, but we've looked everywhere else. Joey is up in the north pasture." Using a pair of binoculars, he searched the hillside, then shook his head and put the glasses in their case. "We might as well head back. There's not even a scrub bush for her to hide behind around here."

Alinda gazed at the countryside beyond the fence. It was nothing like the land immediately in front of them. It was like an artist's palette. Summer's greenery was giving way to autumn's showy colors, the trees a myriad of reds and golds. It was an unusually hot fall afternoon. The temperatures had been in the eighties for several days.

Alinda removed her fashionable cotton camp shirt to reveal a bright yellow tank top and then spurred her horse and turned to Nolan, laughing. "I'll race you to the oak tree."

Nolan was on her heels, never one to turn down a race.

After several lengths, Alinda's horse began to limp and Alinda immediately pulled up, short of the finish line.

She dismounted and soothed the horse's muzzle while Nolan checked for an injury.

Murmuring to the mare, Nolan rubbed her back and flank, then gently ran his hand down the injured leg and examined the hoof. Expertly, he pried out a sharp stone from the frog of the mare's foot. "You better ride with me. I don't think she needs a rider with that bruise."

"Will she be all right?" she asked, following Nolan's suggestion and mounting the gelding with a hand from Nolan, sitting astride the saddle horn in front of him. Her body tingled with the hard pressure of his thighs against her hips.

"Yes." He walked the gelding in a slow rhythmic gait, trailing the mare behind with a loose rein.

The heat of the late afternoon sun and the invigorating ride had Alinda's senses well tuned to Nolan's muscular body pressed against hers.

As for Nolan, he wondered how he was going to keep from making love to her before they reached the ranch. The tantalizing rhythm of their bodies in fine tune with the horse's gait spurred his longing. He picked up the pace a little and his arm hooked around her, his fingers splayed across her ribs to hold her steady.

Alinda smiled up at him with her beautiful rounded eyes full of passion. One hand moved up and down the sinewy length of his thigh, her fingertips creating a maddening friction over his taut jeans.

He planted a kiss on her temple and then he gave his lips free rein to travel down her bare neck, glad the horse knew the way back because he wasn't sure he would be able to concentrate on their direction—in reference to the ranch, that is. It didn't take a compass to know the direction Ali was headed.

His thumb touched the sensitive underside of her

breast, then his hand inched upward to cup the entire sphere. Unrestrained beneath the stretchy top, her full breast swelled, its excited tip responding to him. Her instant reaction quickened his male response. He pressed her back against his torso, against his body's urgent need for her, relieving none of the discomfort or the wanting.

His lips devoured her neck and his teeth nudged the slim strap off her shoulder and nipped at her soft flesh. His hand moved over her in frenzied haste. The heat of her body coursed through him, inflaming his desire. It was unbridled, searing passion that had nothing to do with the heat of the sun on their fevered flesh.

He shifted in the saddle, dreadfully uncomfortable. His hand pulled her against his heaving chest and he forced himself to calm down. "Ali, I've never met a woman who could make me lose my self-control. You scare the hell out of me."

She felt his breathing slow but refused to let him pull away. Driving her fingers through his hair, pressing her head back to his shoulder, she turned slightly in the saddle where she could see he was having a hard time controlling himself. One soft breast pressed against his pounding heart when she pulled his lips down to meet hers.

He tried to resist, tried to summon up the common sense that had buried itself deep within him, but the thick shadow of her lashes fluttered against her cheeks as her tongue boldly outlined his mouth and he was lost to her touch, lost to everything but the wonderful sensations she stirred in him. He drew in a hissing breath and trembled with desire when the pink tip ventured into his mouth, darting across his teeth as the dewy softness of her lips sealed his.

"Stop," he moaned. "Stop." But even as he begged, a

groan of surrender rose from deep in his chest as he matched her ardor, his arm fervently holding her to him, taking the initiative with a kiss full of hunger and need. "We'll fall off," he muttered unconvincingly.

"Oh, Nolan, how much farther to the ranch?"

"So close we're going to have an audience if we don't stop this minute."

Joey ran out to meet them and took the reins of the lame horse. "We found Jezebel's calf. She was caught in the barbed wire of a downed fence. Looks like we're gonna need the vet." His eyes darted from Nolan to Alinda's flushed face and nervously cleared his throat. "I'll take the horses if you want."

"Take the mare. I'll be along shortly." Nolan helped Alinda slide down and dismounted himself. He closed his eyes, trying to force himself to be rational, to act as a responsible adult rather than an adolescent teenager with an overactive libido. If he followed her back to the main house, every hand on the ranch would know what they were doing. "I have to check on the calf." He eyed her expression with trepidation, the passionate embers only tenuously banked, and hoped she wouldn't argue with his decision, barely able to stand by it himself. "It's better this way," he said, addressing her unspoken words. He turned and left her standing outside the barn, leading the quarter horse inside without looking back.

Alinda trudged up the hill to the main house, frustrated and hurt. It all seemed so futile. He wasn't ever going to open up to her. He had had plenty of opportunities and he had always pulled back. The distance he put between them this time hurt Alinda more than it angered her, and she wondered when she crossed the threshold from curiosity to genuine caring and concern.

There were times when he looked at her that she didn't

119

doubt he cared very deeply for her. Then there were other times that the tunnel to his soul seemed so long and dark, she felt she would never be allowed to reach it. And there was always the unbidden possibility that he was simply a male reacting normally to the natural urges of his body when approached by a woman. The thought made Alinda cringe. She much preferred to think he was falling for her as she was for him—fast, headlong, and out of control.

She stripped quickly and took an icy shower. The needle spray washed away her immediate needs, but not her frustration or the deep-seated longing that Nolan had created within her.

After checking on Jezebel's calf and consulting the vet, Nolan caught himself following the path to the main house and veered off toward the corral instead. The more distance he kept between them, the better. He could keep his body away from her, but not his mind. He wondered what she was doing as he leaned against the fence post to have a smoke, a lonely silhouette, nothing to give away his position but the small glow from the tip of his cigarette.

As each light in the house went out, he followed her progress until finally only a small golden glow from the bedroom was left. He took a long, deep drag from the cigarette and raggedly exhaled. What kind of fool was he? She was willing and he certainly couldn't want her any more than he did at this minute—his body literally ached with wanting.

There were two kinds of women: those a man could take pleasure in and walk away as easily as he had come, and those that wove their invisible ribbons around a man, chaining him with satin and lace as binding as any steel shackles. Instinctively, he knew Ali wasn't the kind a man could walk away from after a night of lovemaking and not regret it the rest of his life.

Savagely, he snuffed out the cigarette with his boot, but the flame of his desire wasn't so easily extinguished when the soft glow of the bedside lamp shadowed Alinda through the sheer curtains. He watched, entranced, as she peeled off her clothes and let a wispy nightgown float around her body, the body he had held so intimately only a few short hours ago.

He lifted his hat from his head and knocked it against his thigh, sending dust scattering in the moonlight. He had to do something to get his mind off of her, something to relieve the pressure building in him.

He headed for the pickup, gunning the engine before jerking it into gear and heading down the drive. He knew exactly where to go. Natalie worked at the local grocery. She was pleasant enough to pass the time with, but he had never pursued any of her invitations.

He drove for over half an hour, until he was in the next county, then took a dirt road into the darkened, tree-covered mountainside. The moon had disappeared behind a cloud and Nolan had to slow down, creeping along the rutty road. It slipped out into the open again, throwing the old clapboard house into sharp relief against the dark meadow. He slowed even more before coming to a stop several yards from the house. He let the engine idle, clenching the steering wheel, white-knuckled.

The yellow porch light cast a malevolent glow over the yard. It seemed to taunt him, accusing him of . . . *of what?* he demanded. *Being human?*

The instant of hesitation became minutes as he pondered over his feelings for Ali, staring at, but not seeing the old house. Riding beside him across the countryside, she had become a constant in his life that he was going to find it hard to live without, throwing her enthusiasm into the most mundane projects, drawing a smile from him when he least expected it.

Focusing on the white house, he admitted he didn't want another woman. He wanted Ali. Suddenly the thought of what he was about to do caused a sour feeling in the very pit of his stomach and he couldn't go through with it. He couldn't pretend interest when it wasn't there. Not tonight. Maybe at some point in the future when the ache for Ali dulled. Maybe.

He shifted into reverse and lifted his foot from the brake, making a U-turn in the dirt road. The red needle of his speedometer stayed well below the lawful limit as he returned to his cabin. There was no need to hurry. No one waited for him there.

The past few weeks, he had neglected the mounting paperwork and now he tackled it with a vengeance, fastidiously concentrating on every detail. The desk lamp glowed into the wee hours of morning. He had never felt so alone.

Joey arrived at the main house while Alinda was dressing for her afternoon ride.

"I've got a note from Mr. Taylor for you, ma'am."

"Oh? Thanks," she said distractedly as she tore the envelope open. In very neat, bold strokes, Nolan said he couldn't make their ride for a few days because of some work he needed to catch up on and preferred that she didn't go alone.

"Any reply, Ms. Sterling?" Joey broke into her thoughts.

"No. No reply." She wanted to be mad at Nolan. She wanted to scream at him. If he couldn't be honest with

122

her, at least be honest with himself. He was purposely avoiding her, she was sure of it. Well, if he wanted space, she would give it to him.

She continued to dress, but paused after tugging on one boot. She didn't want to go without him. It wouldn't be the same. She debated whether to go back to Tulsa and quickly negated the thought of giving up so easily. She would wait. When he saw how determined she was, he would come to her. Patience was her best bet.

She hadn't so much as waved to Nolan in three days and she missed him dreadfully. The temperature had dropped considerably and she decided to build a fire in the fireplace. She stepped out to the firewood bin and stacked three logs across her arm. Glancing around the ranch, knowing he was probably within hollering distance, made it all the harder to wait him out.

With a glass of wine in her hand and a warm fire glowing in the fireplace, she settled on the oatmeal-colored rug and an array of soft pillows facing the blazing flames. She loved the unpretentiousness of the ranch. So much so that she was considering selling the house in Tulsa for something less ostentatious. Before leaning back to relax, she removed her boots and wiggled and stretched her toes, then loosened her braid and ran her fingers through her hair, combing and separating the shiny waves.

Nolan walked past the picture window in his cabin, vigorously towel-drying his hair. The sight of smoke from Ali's chimney made him pause, a vivid picture flashing through his mind of her languishing in front of the fire. He dressed quickly and acted on an impulse he tried to justify, but couldn't. He stopped at the main house on his way to the local rodeo.

Over the past few days, the distance he kept between

them had given him enough space to rekindle the anger he felt about her deceit and the fear that the investigator might turn up something. She was no better than a gold digger—out for all she could get and more. Her kind were all alike, never satisfied.

Even with those thoughts fresh in his mind, Nolan still knocked hard on the door and counted to twenty by the time Alinda answered. Her eyes had a decided bedroom slant to them and he cursed the instant flare of desire that licked up from his groin.

"Good evening." Alinda had to fight to keep her knees from quaking under her full wool skirt. She was glad it hit well below her knees and the opaque hose kept her ankles from being affected by the chill in the air—a chill that had nothing to do with the weather.

"I thought you would have gone back to Tulsa," he said in a derisive drawl.

"Did you want me to?"

He tried to lie. He tried to say *Yes, yes.* But the words stuck in his throat. He tried to say, *I want you out of my sight, out of my mind, out of my dreams, and out of my life!* But he couldn't. What was the matter with him? He had been lying for four years and yet when he looked into her face, a face that would make angels sing, something in him melted and wanted to tell the unvarnished truth. And the truth was, he just plain wanted her—in his life, in his arms, in his bed. The truth was he loved her, despite all she was doing to destroy him. He loved her. It was irrational but true.

"I was on my way to the rodeo. Get a jacket and your purse, if you like. You're going with me."

"I'm a little tired. I thought I would enjoy the fire and go to bed early." Alinda struggled to stay in her spot, determined not to give in too quickly. Who did he think he was anyway? He had ignored her for three days and now he was ordering her to go with him. "I'm not one of your ranch hands to be bossed around."

Nolan pushed his way past her. "I said get your coat. We're going to be late as it is."

"I'm not stopping you." She wasn't sure what perverse satisfaction she expected from her mutiny, but Nolan didn't make her wait long to find out.

He hauled her to him and kissed her. It was hard and brief, but no less effective. "There's hardly a soul left out here. Everyone has gone to the rodeo. I won't leave you here alone." A muscle twitched at the corner of his mouth. "And I have to go. It's a good chance to check out the local talent, to see who can handle a horse and who shouldn't even be trying."

Alinda stood on her tiptoes and kissed him; unlike his, it was a tantalizing kiss, a promise of things to come. Then she left him and pulled on the fine soft-leather boots and grabbed a heavy shawl that matched her skirt. But when she started braiding her hair into a neat plait, Nolan's hands thwarted her movements.

"Leave it down. It's beautiful." His knuckles grazed lovingly across her high cheekbone.

"I missed you, too." Alinda admitted openly.

He dropped his hand and grumbled, "I'm late." He strode out the door, leaving Alinda to follow. Damn her anyway! What game was she playing? He didn't like the fact that she had clearly read his thoughts in that brief exchange. If she saw through him so easily, what else had he unknowingly revealed?

Alinda talked pleasantly on the drive to the rodeo grounds, more disturbed by Nolan's monosyllabic responses than she let on.

Nolan parked in a freshly mowed field already filled

125

with mud-caked pickups. It was some walking distance from the arena. Dust rose from the corralled area. Pretty horseback riders, clothed in satin and fringe western outfits, carried glossy flags that flapped in the breeze.

They stopped at the shoot area first. The smell of manure was strong, but Alinda didn't comment. She suffered in silence because the way Nolan's eyes fastened on her made her feel that, somehow, he was trying to prove something to her, but she had no idea what. She stood patiently, pretending to concentrate on the dust-shrouded arena.

"Mrs. Sterling, you know Joey Sands and this is Cy Randall."

Alinda inclined her head, but couldn't speak. Nolan's coldness had cut to the quick when he introduced her so formally. There was something so distant in his tone, a distance that his eyes said was useless to try and breach.

She remembered her manners and smiled a little too brightly as Nolan continued to talk. "Cy helps out when we're shorthanded."

The tall man Nolan had introduced as Cy shook Alinda's hand. "I tried to get Nolan to enter the rodeo. He's about the best roper I've seen in a long time."

"I wouldn't want to steal your best event, Cy," Nolan said.

"A *little* competition would do me good," Cy needled. They all laughed. "I'd better get to the shoot. It's about time for me to get ready."

"It was nice to meet you, Cy," Alinda said as he lifted his dusty Stetson and inclined his head.

With Cy gone, Alinda focused her most becoming smile on Joey. His face turned a crimson red to match his thick head of hair.

126

"Mrs. Sterling and I are going to sit in the stands tonight, Joey. Would you like to join us?"

Although his question was polite enough, Nolan's tone was abrupt. There was obviously something bothering him, and Alinda had a strange feeling it had to do with her. She couldn't think of anything she had said or done that would have put him in this mood. He was the one that had forced the distance between them, said it was for the best. If anyone should be mad, it should be her!

Glancing over his shoulder, Nolan eyed the stranger that had followed their every move for the last ten minutes. It could be coincidental that he had come directly from the entrance gate to the shoot next to where they stood. But a finely honed instinct told Nolan differently. His eyes narrowed with decisiveness. He'd give the guy fifteen minutes to get lost, he thought as he led Alinda to seats near the shoots and the entrance gate. Otherwise, he had to consider some alternatives. The shoot area offered the most cover with its maze of stalls, cowboys, equipment, and horses, but from where the stranger stood, he could easily block that alternative.

Alinda noticed that Nolan pulled his wide-brimmed hat lower on his forehead and didn't speak to anyone as they took the few steps up the bleachers. He had to know most of the people in this small town, yet they made no attempt to speak to him either. A few curious glances, but no friendly hellos. It was all so puzzling.

Covertly, she watched him as he studied the saddle bronc riding event with what seemed like great interest. He was a handsome man in a rough-cut way, with an earthy virility that was rarely found in neatly trimmed hair and a three-piece suit. She had the feeling that a haircut and an expensive suit would alter his looks considerably, but she didn't think she would like him any better. It wasn't his looks that appealed to her as much as his manner. Even though he tried to hide it, he was a very kind and gentle man. It showed in the way he handled the animals and in the way he usually treated her. He gave little away about himself, but when he gave his word, you could count on it. The people who worked for him respected him and so did she. She felt instant remorse for having him investigated.

Suddenly, she knew she wanted Nolan to be the one to tell her the truth. She didn't want to hear it from Robert or some detective. She wanted to hear it from Nolan. Certainly not because she wanted to use it against him, and not even so much out of curiosity, but because she wanted him to trust her, to care for her enough to share it with her. It was a startling revelation about the man that sat so stiff and proud beside her. First thing in the morning, she would call Robert to stop the investigation before it was too late, before she stirred up more trouble than she could handle.

Nolan was hardly aware of the woman so raptly studying him. His eye was trained on a man at the foot of the bleachers. He tried to concentrate on the bronc riding, but it was becoming more and more obvious that it was an exercise in futility. The man was too conspicuous to ignore. The way he continued to stay in the shadows was suspicious in itself, but his lack of interest in the rodeo was plain for all to see.

There was always the possibility that he was the investigator Alinda had hired. He shook his head imperceptibly. He was obviously an amateur and Nolan didn't think Robert would waste his valuable time working with an incompetent detective.

Nolan examined a few other options and settled on the most likely. If it was one of Martinelli's men, they had

128

pegged him and now Alinda too. They weren't moving in, though. That was curious. It must mean they want him to squirm, to panic and do something foolish. He cursed under his breath as his hands gripped the edge of the wooden bleachers, the tiny splinters piercing his fingers unnoticed. He was too wrapped up in berating himself for giving in to the urge to bring Ali along. The corner of his mouth twitched violently.

He consoled himself with the fact that he had been in worse spots, but as quickly reminded himself that just because he had squeaked out of tight situations before didn't give him any guarantees that this would be a repeat. He had never had a woman to contend with before either. She presented a whole bushel of problems.

"Isn't that Cy?" Alinda asked, unaware of Nolan's foreboding thoughts.

Distractedly, Nolan glanced at the shoot area and for the first time in fifteen minutes, he spoke. "Yes, he's the next man out." He didn't look at Alinda, just nodded toward the south end of the arena and the calf erupting from behind the gate.

He had been so preoccupied, he hadn't noticed that the saddle bronc riding had ended and the calf-roping had begun.

Alinda watched, her breath held in her chest as Cy went in pursuit, his lasso circling over the animal's head. In one motion, he wrapped the end of the rope around the saddle and threw himself off the well-trained horse. He flipped the calf over on its side and took a short piece of rope from between his teeth and tied it around three of the calf's legs, then flung both hands high into the air.

"I think that's the best time yet," she commented, trying to strike up a conversation that would keep his interest. She wasn't sure how much longer she could stand his cold withdrawal. How could they work through this if he continued to ignore her?

Nolan only allowed his attention to be snagged by Alinda for the briefest second, then he continued to surreptitiously watch the circumspect stranger. As he observed from the corner of his eyes, his body stiffened, a buzz of alarm trilled up his spine. It was clear they had to get out of here, and fast.

Alinda clutched Nolan's flannel-shirted forearm and leaned over to whisper in his ear, "Nolan?" She had to try to think of something that would break the barrier he had put between them. How could so much distance be placed between two people whose thighs were touching? She felt a stab of guilt. He must know about the investigator. It was the only logical explanation. Why else would he be so cold toward her?

Startled by her sudden closeness, Nolan turned to face her and their lips were a breath apart. Her eyes were huge in her small face and guilt consumed him for not leaving Indian Paintbrush sooner. This could have been avoided if he hadn't been so determined to try and stick it out six more months. Then with the sudden blink of her coal-dark lashes, he was reminded of the part that she had played in all of this. If it hadn't been for her infernal snooping . . .

For an instant, Alinda couldn't speak, couldn't think of why she had wanted his attention. The corner of his mouth twitched and it took every ounce of willpower to pull her gaze from his lips and focus on his eyes. They had a crudely cynical glint in them and it intimidated her more than his violence ever had.

Through gritted teeth, he said, "Let's get out of here. Follow me and don't ask any questions and *don't* look back."

Alinda started to protest, but Nolan reached under her shawl and squeezed her hand in a punishing, viselike grip that brooked no arguing.

It was imperative that they blend in with the crowd as much as possible, he thought as he led her down the steps. Glancing back at her, he laughed humorlessly at the absurd thought. She couldn't blend into this crowd if her life depended on it—and it very well might, he thought grimly.

He watched the man from the corner of his eye, hoping with his whole being that he wouldn't follow them, that his imagination had been working overtime. But his hopes were quickly dashed as the stranger began to move in their direction.

"Nolan, slow down. I can't keep going at this pace." She continued to stumble along in his wake when he ignored her plea.

Roughly, he pulled her behind a concession stand. "Get down," he hissed as he crouched, peering back the way they had come before dragging her down a row of parked vehicles, doubling back to their truck, glancing over his shoulder before letting Alinda inside.

"What is going on?" The intrigue sent her blood pounding excitedly through her veins, but her excitement was short-lived. Nolan's pupils seemed to dilate and swallow her up before he started the ignition. Her question went unanswered.

He kept his eyes on the rearview mirror more than he watched the highway in front of him. He purposely went four miles out of their way before circling back on a deserted road Alinda had never seen.

Nolan parked the truck where it wasn't visible from the main drive. He followed Alinda into the whitewashed house and slammed the door.

She jumped at the unexpected show of rage. Her dark eyes implored him to explain.

"Don't you dare turn those big brown eyes on me." He shook and turned away, determined not to be swayed from his anger. The drumbeat in his temple intensified. It seemed he'd had a headache twenty-four hours a day since she had come into his life.

"Please tell me what is going on. I have a right to know." She had been so caught up in the situation that she had fallen in love with him without realizing it. Didn't he see the love in her eyes?

A frightening, humorless laugh rumbled from deep in his chest. "Tell me, Ali, exactly what is it that gives you the right? The three hundred dollars a day, plus expenses you've paid a detective for three months, to turn up nothing." He turned to glare at her, then scooped up an ashtray and hurtled it into the fireplace. Good God, his life was falling in around his ears and it was all her fault! He wanted to shake her until her pretty, even white teeth rattled. He crossed the room, intending to do just that. His callused hand curved around her upper arm, hauling her against his hard chest, jerking her to her tiptoes. Even the bulky sweater didn't cushion the bruising pressure of his fingers. He glared down at her, his eyes narrowed to menacing slits, his angry breath hot on her face. He was surprised at the satisfaction he derived from the frightened quiver of her mouth. Maybe a taste of what he had been through because of her would be good for her. As he stared down at her, his eyes became a dark, stormy-night blue. The urge to yell at her and make love to her were warring for supremacy and he thrust her away from him in disgust with his own ambivalence.

Alinda bit her lip, her surprise at his knowledge overridden by the desperation she felt. It didn't even occur to

132

her to ask him how he had known. "If you would let me explain—"

"Spare me your explanations. The unembellished truth is that you were too greedy to let Jackson give away even a small piece of his holdings to someone other than yourself. All the tears and the talk of him being taken advantage of was just the first act of the play, wasn't it, Ali?"

"That's not true." She was stung to think he found her so shallow and uncaring. "I don't blame you for being angry."

"You don't blame me?" He repeated, deceptively calm and then louder, "You don't blame me? That's so kind of you," he said sarcastically.

"It's true. At first, I really didn't believe you came by the inheritance honestly. But as I grew to know you better, I realized why Jackson would have liked you and believed that he felt indebted to you."

"You're a creative liar, too. My, my, you are quite a woman, Mrs. Sterling."

She rushed on, his words wounding her more than she would have thought possible. "I know you won't believe me, but I realized tonight how much it meant to me for you to tell me the truth yourself." Tears sprang into her eyes at his implacable expression. "I was going to call Robert tomorrow and have him call off the investigation. I swear it's the truth."

"You don't know what the truth is!" he bellowed, all the weeks of pent-up frustrations bursting forth. "It was all a ruse, wasn't it, Ali? Pretending to care about the ranch, to care about me. All the sweet southern hospitality was just an act to bring me to my knees." He glared at her, coldly challenging her to deny his words. "Tell me, I'm curious. How far were you willing to go to get me to bare my soul? All the way to bed? I wonder what Jackson would have thought of that? His country club wife playing the harlot?"

She had never hit anyone in her life, never even had the urge to, but her hand came around swiftly, too quickly to realize what she was about to do, her hurt pride propelling her into action.

Nolan caught it within inches of his cheek and hauled her against his chest. His grip was crushing around her slender wrist. Their eyes clashed, hers, dark and angry and hurt, his, blue thunderclouds of distrust.

"Mine was no more an act than yours was and you know it."

His eyebrow arched skeptically. "What makes you think I wasn't acting?"

She sucked in her breath. Hot tears sprang into her huge eyes, which were rounded in hurt.

"You've reminded me of a valuable lesson, Mrs. Alinda Sterling. Just because a pretty package is wrapped in silk and satin doesn't mean it isn't full of snakes waiting to strike when you least expect it." He shoved her away in disgust and dropped her wrist. "I believe this is still my property. I'd like you off of it first thing tomorrow." He left her, closing the door with a soft hush.

He tried to hold on to his anger, tried to remember all that she had done to destroy him as he threw his few belongings into a bag. He zipped it up and slung it over his shoulder, fully prepared to leave. But as usual his common sense hammered at the back of his mind and his steps faltered halfway across the room.

Was this really the right thing to do? Or was he panicking without real provocation? Yes, there had been a conspicuous-looking man at the rodeo. Yes, he had certainly appeared to be following Alinda and himself. But Nolan had no actual proof.

If his original theory had been right, and it was actually one of Martinelli's men, the man had not followed them here. Of that Nolan was sure. Here at Indian Paintbrush, he had more security than he would have on an open highway with no backup. If he stuck close to the ranch for the next few weeks, and watched his back, it might all turn out all right.

He slumped down on the bed and thought of the tears Ali had shed; doubts ate away at his soul. Had they been another ploy to bring him down or were they genuine? It didn't really matter anymore, so what was the point in rehashing it?

She would be gone by morning and that was better for them both. Nothing could come of a wealthy socialite and a man with no prospects for the future.

Acute disappointment engulfed him, for an emptiness he had carried for four years and had foolishly let her fill.

CHAPTER EIGHT

"Ali," he whispered in an unguarded voice, at first not certain that she wasn't a dream. No matter how often he reminded himself of her betrayal, the mere sight of her erased it from his mind. The wild jungle print of her shirt reminded him of her dark tiger eyes and her elegant and all too familiar perfume, tantalizingly evocative, provoked an attraction he was far beyond denying.

But, he qualified, that didn't mean he was anywhere near giving in to it, and as quickly as her name slipped from between his lips in surprise, his jaw tightened and his tone grew demanding. "What are you doing here?"

She had been conniving all along, the whole time letting him believe she was abiding by their agreement. She had agreed not to pursue the fighting of the will. Technically, she had not gone back on her word, but as far as he was concerned it was only a matter of semantics. Hiring the detective was, in essence, the first step toward contesting the will, a way to, hopefully, achieve his downfall.

"I thought I made myself clear," he reiterated harshly.

136

"I don't want you here." Who was he kidding? He wanted her more than life itself. He scowled. Why couldn't he look at her and be filled with disgust? How could he acknowledge in one breath her cunning betrayal, and in the next, be consumed with desire for her?

It had been a week since Alinda had seen him; she had hoped that the separation would have given him time to cool off and a chance to miss her as much as she had missed him. Was this really a one-sided relationship?

No longer able to meet his grim, unforgiving gaze, her eyes moved to the corral. She took a deep, shuddering breath, clutching an envelope to her breasts. The horses milled around the fenced area and she was flooded with memories of the rides they had taken together, the good-natured races that left them exhilarated and exhausted, the relaxing walks, with the horses trailing behind them, the day her mare had gone lame and she had had to ride with Nolan . . .

"Well?"

She jumped at his impatient demand. "I came to bring you this." She held out the unopened envelope, trying desperately to keep her hand from shaking, but failed. "It's the report, the investigator's report." She took a deep, nervous breath. "I didn't open it and neither did Robert." There was the barest trace of a tremor in her voice as she continued. "You're the only one who will see it."

His stormy eyes went from the envelope to Alinda. "Besides the investigator, you mean?" he challenged coldly.

She lifted her trembling chin to a proud angle and faced his angry glare. "If you had been completely honest with me, I wouldn't have had to resort to this."

He murmured something she didn't quite hear, but un-

137

derstanding his meaning was not hard—he didn't believe her.

"I can't change the flow of water under the bridge, Nolan."

"No, it's too late for changes," he agreed, smiling with dangerous restraint.

There was more than one meaning to his bleak statement and the finality of it tore at Alinda's heart. She had to think of something fast or she knew she would lose him for good.

"Would you mind if I went riding one more time? I'll be back early enough to drive back to Tulsa this afternoon." Alinda held her breath.

He looked as if he would turn her down. He glanced away and abruptly said, "I'll saddle the horses."

Her hand snaked out to stop him as he turned away. She felt the hard muscles of his forearm flex in surprise at her sudden touch.

"You don't have to go with me," she rushed to clarify herself. "I know you would prefer not to. I won't get lost."

"I've got an hour or two free," he said gruffly, folding the envelope and stuffing it in his shirt pocket before striding into the barn.

He tried to ignore the physical effect she had on him, but it was hard when he couldn't help but notice the way the two pockets on her shirt were strategically placed, or the way it tucked in neatly at her waist, or the jeans that emphasized the pounds she had put on by molding her supple hips and long slender thighs. He gritted his teeth and wondered if he would ever stop wanting her as he led the two saddled quarter horses from the barn.

He helped Alinda mount her mare. "You always look

like you just stepped out of a fashion magazine," he said. "Don't you own any grubbies?"

"These are my grubbies," she said innocently.

He made a mocking sound and mounted his gelding. The saddle leather creaked and the horse danced nervously. Nolan patted and smoothed his neck, talking softly until Thunderstruck was accustomed to the weight on his back.

They followed a cedar-lined boundary fence for half a mile before turning and heading diagonally across the rolling land. Nolan kept a sharp eye and stayed to trails that lent them sufficient cover.

"I'd like to go to the knoll you told me about last spring," she said, after suffering his silence most of the way.

Nolan surveyed the landscape. "It's quite a ride from here."

"This is probably the last chance I'll have to go riding for a long time and you promised to show it to me." Between the lines were the painful thoughts that she would never have another chance to go riding with him.

They stared at each other in awkward silence for several seconds until Nolan nodded and broke the contact, immediately thinking it was a mistake. It was really too far to get back in time to make sure Alinda left for Tulsa today and he didn't like the idea of her traveling alone at night.

When they came upon a line of bare cottonwood trees, Nolan reined in his horse, took off his hat and wiped his face on the shoulder of his shirt. He hooked his hat on the saddle horn and dismounted. "We'll rest here." He couldn't help but grin at Alinda when she winced as she dismounted.

"It doesn't take long to get out of shape," she admitted.

"Would you rather go back?"

"No." She shook her head. If they went back then she would have to leave for Tulsa and leave Nolan. The stiff muscles would be well worth a few more hours of his company.

"I was pretty hard on you last week," Nolan admitted, looking at her over his saddle.

It was his way of apologizing, of meeting her halfway, and she accepted it. Feeling the time was right, she ventured softly, "Why didn't you tell me you knew about the investigator?"

"I thought if I kept it a secret I'd have the upper hand, that maybe you wouldn't be as careful or as wary of me." His smile was dry and humorless, an inner anguish that penetrated his features and arced between the two of them.

He took off toward a large pecan tree, and leaned his fist against its trunk. When Alinda joined him, he captured her hand and played lightly with her fingers, staring off into the distance. Wary and angry as he knew he should be, he still acknowledged that it felt good to be here with her.

She studied his rugged profile, wishing he weren't so complex. She had lived a sheltered life. He, on the other hand, carried a wealth of knowledge and experience on those broad shoulders. She was strong enough to help carry the burden he was hauling around, if she could only prove it to him.

His hand tightened around hers; then he dropped it and leaned down behind her to pick a fistful of late lingering wildflowers. He arranged all but one into a rounded bouquet and thrust them out to her, suddenly embarrassed by his romantic gesture. It wasn't something that came naturally to him, except when he was with her.

She accepted them, deeply touched, her eyes lit with enchantment.

He picked another flower and twirled it between his fingers before running it along the fine line of her cheekbone, then down the delicate cut of her chin and across the full, vulnerable lips that quivered under the petal's softness. He tucked the yellow flower behind her ear and slid his hand around her neck. His lips gently brushed hers, over and over, tasting the pungent wildflower as his thumb whispered around her ear and down her throat to rest on her pulse.

A breathless intoxication filled her at his incredibly gentle touch.

"You're the most beautiful woman I've ever known, Ali. You have a special quality, an eagerness born of innocence, and a freshness, as if mother nature herself kissed you."

"I wish you could understand why I hired the private detective."

"I know why you did it," he ground out.

"I don't think you do."

He stepped back. His body wanted to put distance between them, but his hands lingered on either side of her neck, his thumbs putting the slightest pressure on her chin, forcing her to face him. "Let's not get into it," he said darkly, his voice suddenly husky as he watched the play of emotions on her face. What was the point? They would never see eye to eye. How could he explain his ambiguous feelings? She could have destroyed him, yet he understood and possibly would have even made the same decision had he been in her place. But he wasn't in her position and he found it damn hard to forget what

141

she had done. If she had betrayed him once, what would stop her from doing it again? She said she hadn't looked at the report, but did he dare believe her?

He, who had been in a business that demanded accuracy, demanded that he hone in on a person's intentions and act on it with reason and precision, saw a dozen emotions flit through this woman's eyes and couldn't get a handle on any of them.

Deep down, buried under layers upon layers of thick skin, he knew she wasn't the insensitive, greedy socialite he had thought. He was still angry that she had hired a detective. But the anger was directed more at himself for not moving on when he saw her coming. He knew from the first day in Robert's office that she was going to be trouble, that he was drawn to her in an elemental way that was new to him.

He dropped his hand. "If we don't get started, you won't have time to drive back to Tulsa before dark."

She could only wish. She wanted to scream with frustration. He had been more honest about his feelings today than the whole three months she had known him and yet he had pulled away. With a little more time, maybe they had a chance. Opening her breast pocket, she smiled and carefully tucked the small bouquet of flowers in it.

They rode another half mile in silence, each wrapped up in their own thoughts. A slight breeze had come up and the sun disappeared behind a large dark cloud.

"The knoll is on the other side of that grove of pecan trees," Nolan announced.

"Do you think it will rain?" Alinda asked as a clap of thunder rumbled in the distance.

"Not now, but those clouds in the west are brewing up a real storm. When that cool air hits the warm air we're

142

feeling, it could create a severe electrical storm, maybe even a tornado."

He broke into a trot and Alinda followed at the quickened pace. Their conversational topics had been reduced to the weather, she thought, growing more and more discouraged.

They made their way through a group of scrub oak trees and cantered up the hillside.

Alinda turned her horse to view the way they had come. "Oh! You were right. It's breathtaking, Nolan." To the north, Alinda could see the pond they had fished at during her first visit to Indian Paintbrush, the first time Nolan had kissed her. She looked at him, wondering if he wanted to kiss her as much today as he had then. That kiss had been a gently searching touch. If he kissed her today, she suspected it would be in quiet, passionate desperation.

To the south, she had a panoramic view of the ranch. The buildings dotted the autumn landscape. The trees on the hillside had lost their vibrant color and the majority of their leaves, but the sight still took her breath away. She felt terribly insignificant amid the ancient trees and majestic hills, a mere speck among nature's splendor. This had become home to her. Tears stung her eyes and she forced them away.

With a bright smile on her face, she turned to Nolan, who hadn't spoken since they had stopped to admire the view. He was looking out over the land beyond, his eyes squinting into the brilliant sunlight. His body was tense, poised. "What's wrong?"

He glanced at her quickly as if he had forgotten she was there. "Probably nothing." He dismounted. "Go back to the grove of trees and stay there until I come and get you." His lips were drawn into a straight line, white around the edges.

A silent alarm buzzed through his nervous system when he scanned the area and saw no one.

"Something is wrong," she insisted.

"I'll handle it. Just do as I say!" His voice was sharp, urgent. "And stay there no matter what happens. The trees will keep you partially hidden." Without waiting for her to comment, he slapped her horse on the rump, sending it back down the rise in a trot.

Nolan cursed to himself. He was standing out in the open, with only his horse for cover. Again he scanned the area around the lone bois d'arc tree.

He was sure he had seen a wisp of smoke. He flipped open the saddlebag and lifted out a set of binoculars. Again, his eyes traveled the immediate area. There. He was right. A fire had been doused, and recently too. But there was no sign of anyone. Were they behind that tree? It certainly had a large enough trunk to hide a man. There was nowhere else to hide except the grove of trees and anyone would have had to pass him first. No. He had to be behind the tree, he surmised.

Nolan quickly calculated the odds of forcing a confrontation, but when he thought of Alinda so near by, he decided the risk was too great. He took the time for one more searching look. Nothing. He turned and took in the view that anyone could see from the top of the hill. All but the extreme north side of the ranch buildings were exposed. It was an excellent location. He would have chosen the same spot himself.

Anyone coming or going could easily be followed with high-powered binoculars and no one could sneak up on you unexpectedly. They could be seen coming for miles. Damn! He had thought he was safe here, but hadn't he been running long enough to know that he wasn't completely safe anywhere? He caught the reins of his horse and mounted, hunching into its neck until he was protected by the crest of the hill. Even when he straightened, it was only partially, his back and shoulders tensed and ready for anything as he urged his horse into a run.

Nolan spotted Alinda at the edge of the grove, her hands clasped in front of her, her stance anxious. The usual pink glow was missing in her cheeks; her complexion was terribly pale. Worry lines fanned out from the corners of her eyes and her lips were drawn in a thin line of concern.

"What was it? Are you all right?"

"It was nothing. I'm just a little skittish today. Ready to go back?" he asked, hating himself for frightening her.

She mounted her horse, not believing a word he said. "I saw the way you came off that knoll. It was as if someone were after you."

Laughing, he shifted uneasily in the saddle. "Your imagination is getting the better of you."

His piercing blue eyes twinkled down at her, but Alinda was not fooled. They shone strangely with an alertness, a glimmering instinct for survival.

"It's probably a trespasser. More than likely, some kid hiking across country." Nolan looked over his shoulder one more time. "Have you loosened up enough to race me back?"

Alinda wanted to cover her ears and shriek at him to stop the lies, but instead, she dug her heels into the horse's flanks, letting her actions be her only reply. They cleared the grove of trees and Nolan made sure Alinda took the lead and kept it. He had thought his relationship with Alinda was relatively safe in the remoteness of the ranch, but evidently he had been wrong.

145

They rode into the back pasture, Alinda winning by a nose. But this time there was no joy in her victory. Their footsteps pressed into the soft earth as they dismounted and walked the rest of the way to the barn.

After a hand took the horses, Nolan searched the big thunderheads rolling in. "That storm is moving faster than I thought. You'd better stay here for the night. If it gets bad, hightail it to the cellar. There are candles, matches, and a radio on the left at the bottom of the steps."

"What about you? Where will you go?" Her voice was provocative, teasingly suggestive. She wanted to recapture his earlier mood.

"Cut it out, Alinda," he snapped, fully understanding her insinuation.

His rebuke fueled her own anger. "Are you going to tell me what that was all about?"

He eyed her gravely, the corners of his mouth pulled in a tight, grim line: "I already did." He turned to take the path to his cabin. "I've got paperwork to do," he mumbled over his shoulder.

Refusing to stand back and let him withdraw from her any further, she followed him, reached for his arm, and tried to stop him. "Nolan, don't walk away this time."

"Leave me alone, Ali." He pulled his arm out of her grasp. "I'm sick and tired of your games."

"My games? You're tired of my games?" she repeated incredulously. "You've got some gall!"

"Yes," he rounded on her, unbuttoning his shirt pocket and removing the envelope. "This was some peace offering. I almost fell for it."

"That's not fair. I told you the truth this morning. I called off the investigation."

He ran his hand through his hair in exasperation. "What do you want from me, Ali?"

"I want the truth about yourself, Nolan. I want to know who you are and what kind of danger you're in," she flared. "Is that too much to ask?"

"The more you know, the more you'll be involved. I can't take that chance."

"You think I'm not already involved? I'm in love with you."

His eyes widened a fraction. The corner of his mouth twitched in sharp reaction to her declaration. They had never talked of love, only of caring and needing—and desire. Oh, he knew he was in love with her, but he lived under the misguided notion that she was only using the relationship for her own ends. He grabbed her chin and forced her to meet his eyes, his pupils dilated and searching hers.

"You still don't trust me?" she said in a quiet, hurt-filled voice.

"It's not a matter of trust." He turned and put one dusty boot in front of the other until he was several feet away from her. "Go back to Tulsa in the morning and forget about me," he muttered.

Her eyes were full of pain. "Can you walk away and forget your feelings for me?"

"Given time, yes. I'll forget about you, Ali."

Despite the warm, humid day, goose bumps covered Alinda's body. "I don't believe that!" she cried at his retreating back. "And I don't think you do, either."

Nolan kept walking even as he felt the stabbing truth of her words. His love for her was overshadowing his better judgment. A detective with any experience at all wouldn't have been so blatantly open. Whoever was watching him was deliberately trying to unnerve him and it was working.

He tossed his hat at the rocker on his porch, trying to vent his anger. His hands were fists and one pounded at the porch rail. He swore, a sharp expletive carried away by the autumn breeze. He had lost his ability to be objective where she was concerned, to think clearly and dispassionately in order to take a course of action that was based on experience and reason, not emotion.

At dusk, Nolan found himself watching the main house through his four-paned kitchen window. His brow creased in thoughtfulness as he wondered why Alinda hadn't flipped on any lights. A swift pang of emptiness coursed through him as he realized the dark clouds had blown over and she had probably left for Tulsa. It was just as well. The idea of her being so close for another night was unbearable.

For an instant he allowed himself to relive the way her mouth formed a perfect seal against his own and he wished he had planted just one final kiss on her windburned lips quivering with a mixture of rage and hurt. Oh, hell! He couldn't have stopped after one—not again. Irresponsible or not, he knew he wanted her. All of her. Not just for a night either—forever.

After a dinner he barely touched, Nolan wandered back out to the porch. He felt restless, unable to shake the feeling that someone was watching his every move.

He lit his last cigarette and crushed the package in his hand. He had smoked the whole pack today. He had tapered off considerably until he met Mrs. Alinda Sterling. If the detective didn't get him killed, he'd die of cancer—two decidedly grim alternatives.

He leaned back in the rocker and propped his boots on the rail, one leg crossed over the other. Why did he have

148

to fall in love with her? Why did she have to be as warm as a summer's day in his arms? He couldn't even convince himself it was only lust he felt. It was her whole manner of caring—the way she gave selflessly to others, the way she responded to his every mood.

His thoughts froze when he noticed her car still in front of the ranch house. He felt an instant of jubilation, then as quickly, fear rose in his chest. There were still no lights on in the house. He darted inside his cabin and dialed her number. He ticked off the fifth ring and dropped the receiver on the table with a panicked oath. Terrified that Martinelli had connected the two of them, he ran full speed to the main house. He did not doubt for a second that they would use her to get to him.

Alinda removed the small bunch of wildflowers from her pocket. A tear slipped down her cheek. The memories of their summer flashed through her mind as she found a small vase and filled it with water. The afternoon with Nolan had kept the inevitable at bay for a few hours, but she knew deep in her heart it was over.

She watched in dismay as the pink and orange sun set. But she perked up when Nolan stepped out of his cabin and stood on his front porch. He was a powerful silhouette in the purple haze of dusk. She sighed forlornly and turned away when he went back inside without even a glance in her direction. She held the pungent wildflowers to her nose and breathed deeply. She had received dozens of expensive bouquets in her life, but none had touched her heart the way the miniature burst of color had.

It brought a smile to her sad face. She thought of Jackson and his flamboyant gift giving. There were jewels, furs, surprise parties at the club or at their favorite piano bar, crowded beyond capacity, exotic trips . . .

Her time with Nolan had been so different and she had loved every minute of it. From the shared sunsets to the lingering kiss under the mimosa tree. They had shared something rare. How could he toss it aside?

She carried the vase into the bathroom and set it on the vanity. She filled the claw-footed tub with water and stripped. Its coolness took her breath away at first, but it still felt refreshing. The knobs weren't turned off until the water level passed the swell of her breasts. She stretched out as much as the tub would allow and leaned her head against the porcelain back. She luxuriated there, not thinking, not moving until the shrilling of the telephone jarred her out of her relaxed state.

Determined to ignore it, she sank back down, lifting her toe to catch a drop from the tap, forcing resurging thoughts of the day's events to the back of her mind. She wasn't going to think of it. She was going to relax, clear her mind completely. If he could forget her, she could do the same. She splashed water on her arms and shoulders, then watched it drip off the ends of her fingers, feeling totally relaxed. Closing her eyes, she sank even further, the water lapping her chin.

"Ali!"

Her eyes flew open and she sat up, instantly alert, the water sloshing violently around her. The nickname was endearing and alarming at the same time. She recognized the deep voice immediately, but why was he storming into her house? Half rising, she searched frantically for a towel and bit her lip in frustration when she realized she had to get out of the tub to reach it. She debated, glancing down the hall in a panic. "Nolan?" Her voice was shrill. The tub, filled with crystal-clear water, offered no protection at all. Footsteps thundered in the hall, galvanizing her into action. She rose quickly. The water sloshed around her, droplets cascading down her naked body. "Don't come . . ." Breathless, her words lodged in her throat as she looked up. He was framed in the doorway, larger than life and incredibly handsome.

Shock flared quickly in his blue eyes, but was immediately replaced with admiration. Nolan hesitated only a second before yanking the thick lemon-colored towel from the hook and thrusting it to her. Then he politely turned his back.

"Don't you ever knock?" she demanded indignantly while wrapping the towel around her twice and tucking it between her breasts.

"Sorry. I called and when you didn't answer, I got worried." Hesitantly, he glanced over his shoulder to make sure she was covered before facing her.

"There's no need to worry. I'm perfectly fine."

"Perfect," he nodded, clearing his throat. "I can see that." The raw huskiness in his voice betrayed his own embarrassment along with the deep red creeping up his neck to diffuse his cheeks with crimson.

Alinda couldn't hold back her laughter.

"What's so damn funny?" Nolan shifted one booted foot, then the other.

The towel slipped a fraction and Alinda caught it, but not before the dusky tip of her enticing breast was revealed to Nolan's perusal.

Unknowingly, in that instant, she had completely destroyed what little objectivity he had been able to retain. There was no strength left in him to deny the urges he felt when she stood before him in nothing but a bath towel. Strands of her braided hair hung damply at her temples. Her shoulders were thrown back and her breasts thrust out. The bulky towel hid curves he knew to be there, but not her long, slender legs, legs that he was sure could weave a spell around him he would never forget. His heart beat wildly in his chest. It was insanity. He knew that, but he also knew he was going to make love to her.

He reached across the small space separating them and released the towel. It fell to the floor and she stood before him, a vision of feminine splendor, naked and statuesque.

As natural as the fierce summer sun in August, she closed the distance between them and began to unfasten his shirt, lingering a nerve-wracking amount of time on each button. Her dark eyes never left the passion-filled blue of his, rather feeling her way down his shirtfront until her fingernails grazed his belt buckle. Deftly, she released it and unsnapped his jeans. She tugged the blue chambray shirt free and ran her fingers up his muscled torso and across his chest, curling the shirt in her fingers and removing it from his body.

His chest rose with a deep breath and he exhaled raggedly as she placed her mouth in the springy hair on his chest, and her hands fanned out over his torso. Each fingertip seemed to sear his skin with delightfully erotic pressure.

The soft moistness of her lips covered his chest with tantalizing kisses. They closed over one flat nipple and brought it to life with a single swipe of her tongue. Then she moved to the other one, treating it with the same exciting movement. One sensation after another shuddered through him as her lips followed the patch of hair down his hard belly to its core, heating his flesh as no bonfire could have, pushing his briefs and jeans aside. He felt her smiling against his skin when he took a long ragged indrawn breath and then her even white teeth nibbled at his flesh, teasing and vampishly seductive at the same time, stealing his breath away completely.

His hands gripped the molding above the door until it creaked beneath his unyielding strength as he fully succumbed to her feminine domination. Every muscle, clearly defined in his naked arms and torso, flexed, screaming for release and yet wanting this sweet agony to go on forever. He was lost in the pleasures she bestowed on him, lost in the sheer wonder of the way her loving hands moved on his skin. They ran up and down the back of his hips and thighs. Her lips teased, tormented and satisfied, then made him want more. Her soft breasts made small tantalizing circular motions on his hair-roughened thighs, arousing a raw, searing passion until he could take no more.

He wanted her with such uncontrollable desire it frightened him, desperate for something he couldn't even put a name to. He felt humbled by her beauty and her willingness to make love to him without questions or promises.

He gripped her shoulders, forcing her to end the sweet torment and held her still against him, while he made a concerted effort to slow the blood pounding through his loins. His hands skated down her body, a slow inventory of the shape that had eluded him in so many nights of dreaming. The tempo quickly picked up, a frenzied rhythm in his movements. He paused at the peak of each breast, reveling in the hard, dusty-coral tips his thumb and forefingers brought to life. His journey continued over her ribs and spanned her tiny waist, lifting her up to meet his descending lips. When she willingly arched toward him, his long, bold fingers flared to cover her shapely hips, grasping their soft roundness, pulling her tighter still. His heart raced as she opened her mouth and slid her tongue past his teeth in a passionate kiss, full of hunger and need. His hands began running over her, out of control as the sweet taste of her filled his mouth, his senses. He found her delightfully erotic and wonderfully fresh.

He pulled back and met Ali's eyes, wondering if she could see all his newfound discovery in his eyes, wondering if the feelings were mutual. He felt something akin to worship, thankful she was his to love and to cherish even if it was just for tonight. He drank in the sight of her. In his eyes, she was more than beautiful, she was a gift.

"Tell me how you feel, Ali," he whispered as he held her at arm's length. His eyes searched beyond her obvious passion, trying to grasp the obscure emotions hiding in the shadows of her expression.

"I feel hope for the future for the first time in a very long time. But most of all, I feel loved."

He crushed her to him, pressing her body against the length of his in a moment of desperate indecision. Shaking his head, he moved her away again. "I'm just a temporary diversion. It will pass and you'll go on with your life, with others." His stomach churned at the thought of another man holding her so intimately as his eyes skidded down the peaks and valleys of her feminine figure. "You'll have to." There. He had warned her. Was he warning Ali or himself, he wondered.

"Maybe that's how you feel, Nolan, but don't try to tell me how I feel. I love you and I don't need to pretend or deny it." She could feel his body stiffen. "That doesn't mean there's any obligation on your part to return my feelings. If now is all you have to give me, I'll accept that without question." Her voice shook as she tried to reassure him. "Because I do love you." She put his hand over her heart and it grazed the erotic swell of her breast. "Feel my heart?" Her lips skittered across his shoulder

154

and the sensitive dip of his collarbone. "It's pounding. I want you, Nolan. I want you to love me."

He was so hungry for her, starving for her. His hand moved restlessly over her breast and he was lost. Unable to calm the fierceness of his desire, he crushed her to him. "Let me get out of these damn clothes," he whispered fiercely against her delicate ear before stepping back. He sat down and tugged at his boots and cursed under his breath when they didn't slip off easily.

Alinda stepped over his knee and wrestled with the boot between her legs, provocatively poised in front of him. Her long, slender spine curved into a luscious behind that his hands reached out to steady as she removed the other boot, spurring Nolan's desire beyond control. His jeans slid to the floor in an instant.

Alinda had no time to admire the masculine symmetry of his muscles or the long lean legs that would encase her. He led her toward the bed. Barely controlled passion leaped into his blue eyes as he covered her slender nakedness, the bed springs creaking with his unfamiliar weight.

He wanted to prolong the moments of loving her, of the indescribable sensations as he entered her and meshed his body with hers, but to his dismay, it quickly became an impossible task. Too many weeks had been spent wanting her.

His movements grew faster, and as she rose to meet him thrust for thrust, they grew faster still. He took her fiercely, holding back only long enough to hear her call his name in anticipatory delight.

Once his desire was somewhat sated, he loved her more tenderly, shifting to lie beside her. Worshiping every peak and valley with soft kisses, his mouth reveled in the intimate perusal of her breasts. They molded to his lips just as they had to his hands. He whispered endearments, poignant words of love he had never spoken to another woman.

Relishing her beauty, his eyes followed his hand's journey. He marveled at the perfection beneath his callused hands as they roved over her ribcage, and down into her navel, past her flat stomach. His thumbs stopped to rest, wonderfully, between her thighs and a quiver of ecstasy shuddered through her entire body.

His lips touched sensitive nerve endings. He languished over her for some time, in no hurry to finish the foray, amazed that she was really in his arms, really loving him. Life had had a crazy way of turning upside down on him lately.

His blue eyes met hers and filled with renewed passion as he rolled over and deftly positioned her above him, toes touching toes, thighs to thighs and reveled in her rough cry of passion as he joined them again. He raised his head to enclose the tip of her breast between his teeth, unable to resist as it hung so enticingly above his lips, and then after taking his fill, he nipped his way back up to her mouth, curved in erotic delight, and with an edge of desperation, plundered the riches he found there. Just as he had thought he had taken it all, he selfishly wanted more.

Alinda gently pulled away and straddled his hips, watching his face as he fell back to glory in the feel of her arousing movements and smiled when a moan of sheer pleasure escaped his lips. He wanted her to hold back, to move slowly so they could go on making love forever. But they were both too close. With her head thrown back and her breasts thrust out, her body began to convulse around him and she brought them both to a shattering climax of two hearts searching for a love never meant to be.

CHAPTER NINE

Lying beside him, her breathing calmed and she smiled at him with such contented satisfaction, his heart tripped over itself. With an infinitely gentle touch, he brushed a stray curl from her cheek and she turned on her side, toward him, the lithe body that had made love so passionately now sedately reclined along the length of his. Her arm slid across his chest and her fingers wove in and out of his curls. Her toes, polished a bright tangerine, played with his feet and languishingly teased his calf. It had to be the most luxurious feeling in the world.

He squeezed his eyes shut trying to force reality out as his guilt threatened to overwhelm him. It should never have happened. Never, his mind echoed. He should have used more restraint. What had happened to his self-control? Well, it was too late for regrets. He should leave, cut his losses. But despite the half-dozen reasons he came up with to confirm that line of reasoning, he couldn't summon the willpower to move from her. Even though it was always what he had done before, and never felt a moment's regret for not lingering, he couldn't do it to Ali. Why was she so different? He was trying to make it complicated and it wasn't, at all. She was different simply because he loved her. He hugged her closer and was rewarded with another smile.

That warm, open smile full of gentle persuasion made him want to tell her everything. Her lack of questions motivated him more than the proverbial third degree.

If he was going to put an end to this, he was going to tell her why. She deserved that much. He couldn't let her believe she had meant no more to him than a brief fling. She had insinuated herself into his life in a way that he had allowed no one else, marking him indelibly with her laughter and her love.

"Ali?"

"Mmmm?"

"What I'm about to tell you can go no further than this room. Not to your sister, not to anyone. Not ever." His voice was deep and troubled, yet he was sure of the decision he had made.

Alinda propped herself up on his muscular chest. She had the feeling that what he was about to tell her would irrevocably change their lives. What she had wanted to hear so desperately over the past few months, she was suddenly afraid for him to reveal. The fear showed in her obsidian eyes, in the racing of her heart against his, in the tense, naked body that crossed his.

He touched the anxious pulse in her neck, and ran a long, rough forefinger along her jawline and lovingly kissed her forehead. The story came out, fragmented, at first, then it became his catharsis, flowing out of him like a river dammed too long.

"I was an FBI Agent for eight years. Other than helping my mother run her restaurant, it's about all I knew until four years ago. I was working in Chicago on a billion-dollar drug operation. Under cover, I infiltrated the ring and subsequently gave testimony that led to eighty-seven indictments. One was a kingpin in a major narcotics trafficking operation. He was prosecuted and is now serving a very long prison sentence."

Alinda nodded slowly, her expression a combination of surprise, relief, and confusion. "But I don't understand why you're running. You were doing your job."

The arm that wasn't tracing the smooth planes of her back propped his head up to better see her face.

"He has very long tentacles, Ali. His henchmen would stop at nothing to find me. His right-hand man was never indicted because we couldn't find him. We think he skipped the country. I believe he's back and helping Martinelli run the ring from the joint."

"But the damage is done. Why would they continue to look for you?"

"Revenge." Nolan's mouth twisted upward, a smile full of cynicism. She was such an innocent, he thought.

"Nolan Taylor isn't your real name, is it?"

He took a deep breath. The professional part of him knew this information should never leave his lips, not to anyone—especially to a woman in the aftermath of passion. That's when a man was his most vulnerable. Many female agents had used it to discern critical information. But the other side of him, the side that had trusted no one for his whole adult life, needed to share this burden, this lonely existence, with another human being.

"No, it's not my real name. The government gave me a new driver's license, birth certificate and a passport, along with a pat on the back for luck."

It seemed so very little in return for so much. "And

you've been moving from place to place ever since?" Alinda asked.

He nodded, untangling his body from hers, and left the bed, suddenly restless. Moonlight slithered in from the light-filtering curtains. A chill had crept into the air and Nolan concentrated on building a fire. He crushed the newspapers and mounded the kindling around it, then lit a match to it.

Alinda pulled the sheet up to cover her, letting it rustle around her naked body, at the same time revealing and concealing her womanly figure. As the flames licked toward the chimney, Nolan's bronzed skin reflected the light, his muscles tense and bunching as he worked to fan the flames before settling the larger log on it. She boldly surveyed him in the semidarkness. Her eyes enjoying the journey down his back, over the lean hips and long, hair-sprinkled thighs, a journey her hands had taken and her senses had delighted in.

Her heart went out to him as he stood staring into the fire, a hard yet forlorn expression in his profile. What must it be like to never make lasting relationships? Never to see your family for fear of putting them in jeopardy? Something froze inside her. Did he have a wife somewhere? Children? It was several seconds before she could ask him the plaguing questions and only after she had beckoned with her arms and the soft whisper of his name to return to her.

"Are you married, Nolan?" There was a slight tremor in her breathy question.

Squeezing her tightly, he shook his head and settled her more comfortably against his side. He felt her relax in his embrace. "I've never been married to anything but my work. It wasn't a career that allowed a man to settle

160

down in a house in the suburbs, with a wife, three kids, and a dog."

She was relieved, yet saddened at the same time. "Why did you do it?" she asked with a voice full of anguish over their bleak future.

"I had no family, and no prospects for one. You must understand, Ali. They are the very worst kind of criminals. These people would give drugs to kids to experiment and once the kids were hooked, they told them they had to pay for the drugs if they wanted any more." He stirred to face her, his brow knit in anger. "We're talking about eleven- and twelve-year-old children," he reiterated passionately.

"Are you sorry now that you didn't choose a family over your career?"

"It's too late to be sorry. We do what we have to do."

"Was the story about your meeting Jackson the truth?"

"Yes."

"Did he know about you?"

"No, at least not in the beginning. If he ever found out, he never let on." He shifted one arm across her shoulder and down her back, his hand tantalizingly familiar at her waist, fitted her body along the length of his. "While we waited for the rescue team, we had a lot of time to talk." He dropped a feather-light kiss on her temple and ran a hand over her rounded hip. "He mentioned the ranch and we talked at length about the trouble he was having putting it in the black. I made a few suggestions. I guess he liked them and offered me the job of running it. I'm sure gratitude played a large part in his offer also."

"So you came to Oklahoma."

"I'd been in Colorado for over a year and Jackson offered a steady income at a relatively isolated place. It seemed like the perfect solution."

161

"Until his widow started snooping around." Alinda insinuated herself more snugly into the crook of his arm and ran her fingers through his curly hair. "Oh, Nolan, you must have been horrified to find out I was having you investigated. Did you hate me?"

"I wanted to wring your neck!"

"How *did* you find out?"

"I overheard a phone conversation between you and Robert."

"Oh," she breathed dejectedly.

He hugged her against him. "We have to take the bad with the good." He stroked her love-tousled hair. "If you hadn't been curious about me, I wouldn't be holding you now."

Nolan caressed and stroked her as he answered a few more questions as openly and honestly as he dared, for her own safety. He began to punctuate his answers with kisses, his caresses growing more and more intimately arousing until she was returning them. "You're the most beautiful woman I've ever known, Ali. I've wanted you ever since I saw you in Robert's office, all pale and wan. You were like a delicate flower that needed to be trimmed and put in fresh water."

"I looked positively awful."

"You couldn't look awful if you tried." His hands molded her breasts and brought them to life with the circling motion of his callused palms and they were quickly in the throes of passion once again. He didn't think he would ever tire of her love and attention, even if he could give himself the chance.

"You're like a lighted candle inside me," he ground out, his tone thick with desire. "The more I try to put it out, the more it consumes me, the more I try to put you out of my mind, the more my thoughts turn to you, the more I want you." His voice was almost a groan as he took her lips and ravaged them, moving down on her body, tempestuously sweeping them both into oblivion.

He was fascinated by the way her body fit so perfectly next to his, by the way her hair fanned out in sharp contrast over the wings of her shoulder blades, by the fingers that could taunt and tease his flesh into ecstasy.

"What's going to happen to us?" Ali asked after their breathing returned to normal.

Us? "Shhh. Get some sleep, love." Sanity had returned in a jarring instant. He couldn't tell her that they would never be an *us,* that they would never have a future together. All they would ever have was tonight and that would have to last them a lifetime.

Nolan berated himself for giving in to his emotions. Her coal-fringed eyelids fluttered shut, snagging his attention. What power did she have over him? With one look, she could eradicate his common sense. He waited until she was asleep before extricating himself from her embrace and slipped from the bed to dress. It was imperative that he get back to his cabin before dawn. He couldn't take the chance on someone seeing him leaving the main house in the morning. He had done enough damage for one night. Besides, he needed a few hours' sleep before investigating the trespasser.

He moved around the room gathering his clothes and sat down at her vanity to slip on his socks. He surveyed the array of makeup and creams and picked up a jar, curiously screwed off the lid and sniffed the sweetness. He dipped his finger in the whipped-cream-like substance and rubbed it between his thumb and fingers, sampling its perfumed fragrance again. He would always remember Alinda smelling like this; it would bring to mind a thousand memories.

Despite his quietness, Alinda was awakened. When he reached the door, his boots still in his hand, her voice steeped with disappointment, she challenged him. "Running again, Nolan?"

Stopping instantly, he answered without turning around to face her. His voice was sad, but resigned. "Go home, Ali. Go home and forget you even knew a man called Nolan Taylor."

"And will I be so easily forgotten?" she whispered to the dark shadow of his back.

"It's the only possible solution."

She turned away from the door, not wanting to see him walk out and shivered when the latch clicked behind him. How could he have planned to slip out without a word after all they had shared?

She let him leave without an argument because he had given her a lot to digest and she was more than a little frightened. He was involved in something that she had never been exposed to, seen horrors she could not even begin to imagine. She loved him, but she needed time to think, time to decide where they could go from here.

A hard ball knotted and grew in Nolan's stomach as he entered his cabin. It was hard to breathe over the lump in his throat. He didn't turn on the lights because that might alert someone to the fact that he had just come in.

He cursed his fate and then his government for not resolving this case before now, then himself for remaining in the United States. He was unwittingly being used as a target to capture the few men left in the organization. Whether that's what he had originally intended or not, that was what had happened and he was sure his fellow agents had been intelligent enough to figure it out. He had made it tough for them, though, constantly on the move and rarely keeping in touch with his contact. The contact had been set up for emergencies and Nolan seldom met with any situation he couldn't handle. The last time he had talked to Baker, he had assured Nolan that the case was coming together. But Nolan had been in the business long enough to know that the best-laid plans all too often went awry at the most inopportune time.

When the decision to take their offer was made, he had been thirty-seven years old and never known the kind of love he felt for Ali. How was he to know she would come along when it was too late to change the course of his life?

He looked out the back window and contemplated what might lie beyond the grove of trees, hoping against all odds that his deep-seated fears would be unfounded, that it would be a harmless trespasser. It was a finely honed instinct that told him otherwise. Someone was up there, all right, and he'd be willing to bet they weren't harmless, only watching and waiting for the right time to strike and he intended to be ready.

He needed sleep, but he felt tense and irritable, ready to spring at the slightest movement. There would be no more waiting for them to come to him. He began to formulate a plan. Carefully, he moved across the dark room and found a map of the ranch and a pencil. With one hand along the wall to guide him, he went into the bathroom where there were no windows and closed the door before switching on the light. He stuck the lead of the pencil in his mouth, studying the map with a keen thoroughness before marking every road, path, and trail that would gain access to the hillside where he had seen the trespasser. After great deliberation, he decided on the best approach, folded the map and hid it in his boot.

He threw himself across the bed, fully clothed, except

for his boots. Although exhausted, his mind wouldn't turn off. He rolled over and over again before falling asleep.

. . . A beautiful lady with huge sad eyes entered his bedroom through the closed window, ethereal. More than anything, he wanted to hear her laughter, like windchimes swept unexpectedly by a cool breeze, to hold her without guilt or remorse. Once she had his attention, she ran from him to the far side of the farm pond.

She implored him to come across and then her graceful arms extended to beckon him. The closer he got to her, the farther back in the willows she went, as if someone were using her to lure him. He frantically skirted the pond, trying his best not to lose sight of her in the fog-shrouded willows. All he could see was her black hair gleaming through the moonlit trees. Once he lost sight of her altogether and her scream pierced the still night. He thrashed through the weeping willows, calling her name over and over. "Ali, Ali . . ."

Nolan sat up with a start, his palms sweaty. After blinking several times, adjusting to the dark room, he realized he had fallen asleep and his unconscious had visually drawn out his worst fears. He ran his palm over his face and shook his head, trying to rid himself of the nightmare. His body tensed with apprehension. He should have never let their relationship progress so far. If anything happened to her, he'd never be able to forgive himself. He ached to see her, to know she was unharmed. His heart pounded with the desire to hold her and feel the beauty and the wonder of her in his arms, to know the security only she could offer. He cursed aloud and it echoed through the tiny room. He had lived without a woman for the past ten years. There was no need to start getting soft in the head at this stage in the game. He closed his eyes and dozed lightly. Despite himself, there was a smile on his face as he thought of Ali and the night they had shared.

The moon set low in the sky when Nolan slipped from his cabin and saddled Thunderstruck by the fluorescent beam of light that barely lit the horse's stall. He walked the gelding out of the barn and took a tree-lined path to the pond. It was not the most direct route, but it was the only one that afforded him any cover. He circled the willows that had plagued his nightmares and tied the horse to an old oak on the far side of the pond.

He moved stealthily across the meadow on foot, the moon guiding his way, and positioned himself to watch the stranger at the top of the hill. He couldn't take the chance on moving any closer without being heard. It seemed even the owls were asleep. There wasn't a sound as the sun began to peek over the far mountain, hues of pink and yellow fanning out across the horizon. After an hour of surveillance, there was still no movement from the hilltop.

He waited, in the same cramped position, for another hour. Anyone paid to watch him should have been awake at dawn. He was about to decide there was no reason to continue the vigilance when he saw a movement.

Two arms stretched toward the cloudless sky. A long, lean, uninhibited body followed. Through the binoculars, it was clearly a young man. Nolan took a deep cleansing breath, somewhat relieved.

Quiet as a deer, he made his way through the meadow, pausing once to hide behind a smattering of trees to observe the kid for a moment before continuing to the knoll. It was possible the kid could be a decoy. Nolan focused the binoculars and searched the area thoroughly before approaching the boy. Less than two feet away from the young man, he cocked his rifle and aimed at the trespasser.

The kid turned with a start and stammered, "D-don't shoot, mister."

"Get your arms over your head, kid."

Two skinny arms shot into the air without hesitation. "Geez, mister, you scared me to death pointin' that gun at me. I don't mean no harm. How'd you ever learn to sneak up on people like that?"

Deliberately ignoring the boy's questions, Nolan asked, "Do you know you're on private property?"

"Uh, to be honest, yes, sir. I do, but like I said, I don't mean no harm."

Nolan looked around. He felt more than a little foolish. The kid was obviously telling the truth. He was shaking from head to toe. "Pack your things and clear out."

"I just wanted to get away from the folks for a while. I haven't hurt anything," he rambled as he threw his gear into a duffel bag. "I even ate my beans cold last night. I didn't want to take a chance on no fire spreadin'."

Nolan eyed the young man curiously. "How long have you been here, boy?"

"My name's Hugh Bartow and I ain't no boy. I'm seventeen. I been here since about dusk last night."

Lifting his rifle, Nolan took a menacing step forward, as if preparing to use it. "Don't lie to me. I saw you here, myself, yesterday afternoon."

"No, sir!" Hugh shook his head adamantly.

After a lifetime of rifling the truth out of people, Nolan had no doubt that Hugh was telling the truth. "Did you see anyone else around?"

"No, sir. Just me."

Nolan gave Hugh a curt nod and warned, "Next time

you better pay attention to signs posted or you could get yourself into a lot of trouble."

"Yes, sir." The boy's head was bobbing agreeably as he hurriedly pulled the string on his bag and tossed the meager belongings over his head. "I'll be on my way."

Whoever had been there yesterday afternoon had cleared out. Had it been someone spying on him and reporting back this minute? Or was it just another boy yearning for the wide open spaces?

He wanted to believe the latter, but he knew there was real danger in becoming too lax. There was almost nothing as dangerous as taking his surroundings for granted.

He found the small triangular piece of ground that had been reduced to ashes. He squatted and ground the ashes between his thumb and forefinger. He stood and kicked a rock. Damn! Who had been here? He should have checked it out immediately. Again he had let his emotions dictate his common sense, and it could cost him his life.

He walked every inch of the hillside, searching for a sign, anything that might give him a clue. A stretch of grass about six feet by two feet was still matted down. Probably a sleeping bag. And it wasn't the same place the kid had been sleeping. If this were a movie or a good detective novel, he would find a matchbook cover or lighter with initials on it. But it wasn't a movie, it was his life and there wasn't a clue in sight. For all he knew, it could have been an agent.

He made his way back to the tree where Thunderstruck was tethered, going over the day he and Alinda had gone riding, trying to remember anything that he hadn't thought of already.

The ride back to the ranch was a long one. Nolan was tired. Tired of running. Tired of hiding.

169

"You were out and about early this morning, Mr. Taylor." Joey was in the barn mending a harness when Nolan rode in. "You been hunting?"

"Yeah." Nolan wasn't in the mood to talk. "Take care of Thunderstruck for me. I've got some paperwork to do. If you need me, I'll be in my cabin."

"Sure thing, Mr. Taylor."

Nolan leaned the rifle against the kitchen wall to unload after he cleaned up. The tough leather boots he wore echoed in his cabin as he crossed the wooden floor. He paused in mid-stride, a frown of concentration pinched deep between his brow. There was glass on the oak-planked floor beneath the window across the room. A window shade wasn't hanging precisely the way he had left it, either. It was touching the seal and cupped under, as if someone had pulled it down from the outside.

His trained eyes searched the room, and found evidence that the room had definitely been searched. Carefully, he slid along the wall, wincing when the old floor squeaked. He slowly pushed back the bedroom door, all the way to make sure no one was waiting behind it. He peeked around the molding and surveyed the room. There was nowhere to hide except on the other side of the antique chifforobe and of course under the bed. Damn! Why hadn't he picked up the rifle?

He backed out of the room and retraced his steps to the kitchen. He was pretty sure no one was here now, but he wasn't totally satisfied and he wasn't going to surprise anyone empty-handed. More than likely, *he'd* be the one surprised.

With the rifle in hand, he dropped to his belly and inched his way across the floor, avoiding the squeaking board. He could see under the bed and there was no one. He slid back out of sight and stood to make his move toward the chifforobe. Again, there was no one. He let out a long, pent-up breath. He was getting too old for this.

Nolan began searching the cabin for signs of pilfering, a dreadful foreboding working its way up his spine when he found nothing missing. His eyes fell on the desk and he rushed to it. Sitting down, he jerked open the drawer and in his haste pulled it completely out, spilling part of the contents. He knew it was the only thing that held any information that might confirm their suspicions: the clipping from the ball with his picture. He made a frantic search and exhaled a curse when he saw it was missing. Why had he kept that damn article? Why? His fist formed a tight ball and pounded the desk top. They would surmise that he was emotionally involved with Ali, and they would be right, he thought grimly. If they couldn't get to him, they would use her. He felt an icy tremor race up his spine at the thought.

He picked up the phone and dialed Alinda. He felt an overwhelming need to talk to her, to protect her and be protected, as if only she could calm the pounding of his heart, soothe the uneasiness he felt to the very marrow of his bones. It wasn't until she answered the phone that he realized the full ramifications of what he had done.

"Sorry, wrong number," he muttered brusquely. What was he doing? Was he losing his grip? All common sense flew out the window when he thought of her.

He quickly searched the phone for a tap and then the desk, the light fixtures, the mantel, everything. When he finished, the room was a shambles. Martinelli's thugs had left it neater than he had.

He made a pot of coffee, dishing two extra spoonfuls of grounds from the tin, and stared at it until it perked and startled him out of his dazed state. After pouring a cup,

171

he sipped the thick black liquid and ran a shaky hand through his hair. The wall supported his weary body as he closed his eyes tightly against the unbidden finality of the situation. He knew what had to be done. There was no getting around it. He cared too much for her to allow her to be embroiled in the life that had been carved out for him. He had to get his feelings for her under control and examine his every move with complete objectivity. He had put her in a great deal of danger. The more distance he put between them, the better off she would be. He only hoped it wasn't too late.

CHAPTER TEN

Alinda had jumped with anticipation when the phone rang, only to shake her head in puzzlement when the caller had apologized and hung up. She replaced the receiver thoughtfully, sure the caller had been Nolan. She had desperately clung to the hope that he would realize how much he needed her and he had given in to that need, yet he had changed his mind at the last minute.

Was she going to give up so easily and return to Tulsa as he had ordered her? If he was going to live the rest of his life without her, he was going to tell her face to face, in no uncertain terms, one more time.

The barn was her first stop and Joey had informed her Nolan was at his cabin. The wide-open spaces mocked her as she took the familiar trail. Barren brown and gold fields surrounded her, signifying the end of a growing season, the end of the year. But not the end of her and Nolan! She refused to be pessimistic. It had never been in her nature to look on the dark side and she wasn't going to start now.

The chilling wind whipped at her jacket and she paused to zip it up. She had already lost the first love in her life and she wasn't about to lose the second—not without a fight.

There was no answer to her light knock on the screen door. She peered through the door and could barely make out his figure in the bedroom through the gray mesh. He must have heard her knock. Why was he ignoring her? She knocked again and pulled back the screen, softly calling his name after inching open the door. Suddenly she was confused and uncomfortable, not sure what to say or do at the sight of his packing.

The purpling shadows of early winter storm clouds hung over the ranch, ominously darkening the interior of the cabin. She was stung by the uncompromising rugged profile as he continued to remove clothes from the chifforobe and deposit them in a suitcase.

Why wouldn't he face her? Was it guilt? Alinda tried to sound calm, matter-of-fact: "Where are you going?"

"I don't know." Inwardly, he ached to take her in his arms, but he refrained. Even though she said nothing, her eyes shrieked "why?" Her silence was unbearable. It crawled along his nerves, accusing him of unspeakable atrocities. He tossed his shorts into the bag and returned to the antique closet. His staying here was putting both their lives in danger, there was no denying it any longer. He could stay for six more months and the case still might not be solved. He had to lead them away from the ranch and away from Ali. He would make it so easy for them there would be no need to follow Alinda.

He couldn't give in to the hurt look in her huge doe eyes. He couldn't!

"Don't you want to know why I stayed?"

"It doesn't matter, Ali."

174

"It doesn't matter that I love you, that I would go to the end of the earth with you, if you would only ask?"

He walked around the bed and picked up an envelope and removed a document. "I was going to mail this, but since you're here—" He resumed his packing. "It gives you the authority to dispose of the ranch in whatever way you wish. Donate the proceeds to your favorite charity. Cy has consented to run it until you make other arrangements."

"I don't want this. I don't . . ." She stopped in midstream when she noticed the date in the top left-hand corner. "This is dated a few days after Jackson's will was read. You always planned to leave, didn't you?" When he didn't answer, she pressed louder, "Didn't you?"

He answered her in kind, his tone running angry and deep. "Yes!" He yanked several shirts from their hangers and began tossing them haphazardly into the bag.

"What are you doing?" she shrieked, near panic. When he didn't stop to look at her, she crossed the room and jerked the shirts from his hands, then picked up several items from the suitcase and flung them out. "Stop this! Stop it now!"

He grabbed her trembling hands and turned her to face him.

"I don't understand what's happening here. Was anything you said the truth? All those whispers of love . . ." Her voice broke. "Did you just say them to get me in bed? Was I just one more conquest to be cast aside when it was time to move on?"

"No! God, no," he said vehemently. "You can't believe that." Cursing under his breath, he embraced her. "This wouldn't be so hard if I didn't love you." He stroked her hair and held her to his chest, her tears soaking the pocket over his heart, his burning his eyes. "I'm so damn

175

scared for you, Ali." He buried his face in her neck and inhaled deeply; the familiar perfume she wore was tantalizing as ever.

"So you're scared." She looked up at him, her face tear-streaked. "You think I'm not?" When he started to speak, she pressed her fingers to his lips. "Loving means sharing everything, not just the good, but the bad also. Give us a chance." Suddenly bold, she said, "Let's go away together."

"Are you crazy?" For a few seconds, he had reveled in the feel of her in his arms, the taste of her fingers on his lips, the fierce protective love he saw in her eyes, but her suggestion brought him back to reality with a thud. "Have you forgotten the man at the rodeo or the incident on the knoll?" He ran his hands through his hair impatiently. "These people aren't playing games. That's what my life is like—always looking over my shoulder. You don't want any part of that, believe me."

"We can start over. With my money, we could buy our own island if we wanted, a lush tropical paradise where we would never have to run again." Breathless, she waited frantically for his answer.

"I'm fresh out of hopes and dreams and happily-ever-afters." Leaning his forehead against hers, he continued, "I'm trying to be realistic and you don't make it any easier. When you look at me like that, every rational thought flies out of my head. But not this time, Ali."

Nolan removed Alinda's hands from his forearms, contemplating the impressions her nails left in his skin as he turned away, with seeming indifference, from the only woman he had ever truly loved. He wanted to tell her she had brought to life dreams that were buried so deep he hadn't realized they pulsed within him. Emotions that few men ever knew in their entire lifetime, he had been privileged to feel stir inside him with just one look from her dark eyes. She had soared with him to heaven and then brought him, gently, lovingly, back to earth. He could be satisfied with the short time he had spent with her. But as hard as he tried, the words that rose so easily from his heart could not leave his lips. Rolling off his tongue they would only sound either foolishly romantic, or confused and incoherent.

After gathering the strewn clothes and repacking them, he fastened his suitcase and lifted it off the bed. His eyes roamed over her, remembering the long legs entwined with his as naturally as her silken hair formed a braid and snaked over her shoulder to lay against her right breast. The stricken expression on her face was the very worst of it—an image he would never be able to erase from his mind. He hadn't deliberately set out to hurt her.

He searched again for the right words, the words that would make her understand, but none came to him. Looking directly into her eyes, he willed her to understand how much it was hurting him to leave her and not to hate him after he was gone.

"You don't have to do this," she said, almost hysterical. "Give yourself time to think. You have a choice this time!"

"There are no choices," he said emphatically. "For your sake, it has to be this way. Don't make it any harder than it already is, Ali!"

Defeated, she vowed, "I'll always love you, Nolan."

He gripped her hand to emphasize the importance of what he was about to tell her. "Go home, Ali. Go back to Tulsa where you belong and don't come back. It's too dangerous, too isolated here at Indian Paintbrush." He caught her chin between his thumb and forefinger, forcing her tear-stained face up to meet his piercing blue gaze. Swallowing the lump that grew in his throat with increasing rapidity, he said, "If you love me, you'll do as I say."

When she tried to turn away without consenting, his fingers bit into her chin with firm resolve. Refusing to be swayed, he pressed, "Promise me."

She nodded and turned her back when he dropped his hand, unable to witness his passing through the door, her fist against her chest, holding in the sob until the door whispered shut and his footfalls were no longer heard on the wooden porch outside. Only then did the cry rip from her throat in a painful rush.

She fell across the bed and cried. It was so unfair. Why had fate thrown Nolan Taylor in her path? What had she ever done to deserve such misery? Eventually the tears dried. She wandered through the three-room cabin, momentarily sitting in his favorite chair, fanning through his latest magazine, recalling subjects and anecdotes he had read aloud to her.

She stepped out on the porch, panting when even the fresh air didn't relieve the suffocating strain of losing him and did exactly as she had promised.

Nolan drove for over an hour, mindless of the direction he was headed, Alinda's final sobbing echoing in his head. Utter desolation was the only way to describe the way he felt upon leaving Indian Paintbrush. He had been faced with a lot of tough decisions in his life, but accepting this overwhelmingly inevitable fate was by far the toughest thing he had ever had to do. Logic decreed that he cut his losses, even if Ali was one of the casualties, even if it hurt clear through to the very bottom of his soul.

Several hours passed as Nolan avoided the main highways and toll roads until he could formulate a plan. No longer able to hold it in, his inner frustration finally exploded. "Damn logic to hell and back!" He made a U-turn and headed north, sticking to back roads, finally stopping to use a pay phone. He dug in his pocket for change and rifled through it, counting out approximately what he would need. He paused before inserting the first quarter into the slot. Did he really want to do this? If so, there was only one man he could trust, his assigned contact with the old life. Once the wheels were in motion, it would be impossible to turn back. The quarter clinked into the machine and Nolan had a dial tone.

"Hello."

"Taylor here."

"Taylor, where the hell have you been? I've got half a dozen men scouring the countryside for you."

So, he had been right, after all. They had been keeping very close tabs on him. "You were hoping to use me to shut down Martinelli's operation completely, weren't you, Baker?"

"Yeah. What put you on to us?"

"I guess I always knew it. Otherwise, I would have left the country four years ago."

"We almost had them, Taylor. Our source told us they had found you and were fixing to make a move. What tipped you off?"

"They stole something from my desk, something that only had sentimental value to me. It was a picture of myself and a woman."

"Alinda Sterling?"

Nolan's eyes narrowed and the nerve in his jaw twitched violently. "Yes." If Baker knew about Ali, then you could bet Martinelli knew also. "Baker, you've got to get a man over to Yorktown and twenty-seventh—"

"We've had Mrs. Sterling under surveillance for days now. If they make a move for her, we'll get them."

Nolan's mind worked furiously. "We've got to do something to divert them. They'll go after her." He squeezed the receiver, almost crushing the plastic.

"I was hoping you would say that." The agent told Nolan the plan the bureau had worked out and waited for his input.

"All right. But I want a plane waiting for Alinda and myself. When this is over, I want to make sure she's well out of the line of fire for a few months."

"By then, we'll have Martinelli's whole operation shut down. They know we've got an informant willing to testify as long as we have Martinelli's right-hand man, Angelo Bianco, in custody. He's been in hiding, but we think he'll come to Tulsa to make sure there are no foul-ups."

"They want to kill me to show what they do to traitors and so far I've proven their retaliation efforts to be weak."

"Exactly. If they get to you and we don't arrest Bianco, our informant says he won't testify. We figure Martinelli has put the screws to Bianco. This is his last chance to prove he can handle the business."

Quiet for a second, his mind on Alinda's safety, he considered the worst possible outcome. "Baker, if I don't make it, you make sure Mrs. Sterling is on that plane with a bodyguard."

"It's a deal."

"I should be at the ranch in a little less than an hour."

"Good luck."

Nolan pulled up in front of the cabin, his pulse racing. He was definitely getting too old for this, he thought as he climbed the porch steps. He would be glad when it was over. These men were the scum of the earth and he was going to do his best to nab them, but then he was going to live a normal life.

He glanced around, finding nothing out of the ordinary. He flicked the light switch and quickly but carefully searched the cabin's three rooms. He found no one and no signs of anyone having entered while he was gone.

He rumpled the bed and made it look as if someone were in it using extra linens from the chifforobe. Satisfied with that task, he turned out the light and waited, his body poised, ready to strike.

Baker had been right. Within two hours Nolan heard the knob on the front door turn and click open. There was more than one—two, possibly three people crossing the threshold.

Not a single muscle so much as twitched, even though his body was feeling stiff and cramped. He wasn't even aware of breathing. It seemed he had spent half his life in this position, he could do it a little longer. He hoped they laid rounds of ammo into the lump on the bed without checking the body. If they decided to take him and dump him somewhere, the plan would go awry. There would be no chance of taking them by surprise.

The whelping sound of the gun's silencer made Nolan cringe, his muscles tense in further awareness, knowing the bullets were meant for him.

"Come on, let's get out of here," one of the intruders grumbled.

"Not until I check the body," another one said.

"I pumped a whole round into him. There's no way he survived that."

"I'm going to check all the same." He began walking toward the bed.

CHAPTER ELEVEN

Several hours past midnight, Alinda was still sitting in her study, the pages of her book long since a blur in her lap, her eyes closed of their own volition. Without conscious thought, she drifted off to a dream-filled and troubled sleep.

Her eyes flew open and she sat up instantly, not sure what had awakened her until a knock on the back door startled her. She froze and then looked at her watch. Who would dare come at this hour? Could it be Nolan? Had he come back? Or was it the men after him? Of course not. They wouldn't bother with the formality of knocking.

Nervously, she stood and hurriedly crossed the hallway into the den and peeked through drapes that covered the french doors.

There, in the shadow of the gaslight, she saw him. His familiar figure made her heart stop. She thought she had drained all her tears, but her eyes welled up with tears of joy. Her fingers fumbled with the dead-bolt locks and threw the door open. She ran into his arms, unbelievable relief flooding through her at the sight of him. Arm in arm, she led him into the house, her eyes glowing, her heart bouncing euphorically around her chest.

In the dim light of her den, she could see the devastated look on his face, the tired circles under his eyes and the dried blood on a cut at his forehead, neatly sewn with three stitches.

"What happened?" Stunned, she searched the rest of his body, running trembling hands along his arms. "Are you all right? Where have you been?"

Nolan laughed, a cheerful foreign sound that rumbled from deep in his chest. She wasn't giving him a chance to answer. He felt lighter than air as he pulled her to him and whispered in her ear, "I love you." He pulled her even closer to him. "The rest can wait." His head descended as he stretched her to her toes to meet him halfway. His mouth was firm and strong against the pliant softness of hers. Their passion was all-consuming as they put the harsh words and the hours of separation behind them.

A moan escaped his mouth, searing her lips as he pulled her closer, crushing her breasts against his chest.

She didn't question his declaration. It was a tenuous start and she wasn't going to press for answers. There was a tremendous difference in the man that held her now and the man that had walked out on her hours earlier. He was relaxed, a sparkle of contentment in his clear blue eyes. They were no longer stormy and brooding. She gave herself up to his caresses, her body melting as his warm hands roamed over her breasts and down the flatness of her quivering stomach, then raced back up the lone zipper that kept her nakedness hidden from him.

183

He paused, his eyes searching hers for consent to let him enjoy her body, to love her beyond distraction.

"Let's go upstairs," she invited.

Without hesitation, he swung her up into his arms, her robe flowing sensually across the arm that held her thighs.

She scattered light kisses across his chin and neck, then outlined the strong shell shape of his ear and smiled when his hold tightened and his step faltered.

"Careful, or we'll never make it to the bedroom," he warned.

"It's the double doors to the left," she instructed, in an intoxicatingly breathless voice, at the top of the winding staircase.

He let her feet slide to the floor, ever so slowly, sucking in his breath when her hips brushed against him. He watched, mesmerized, as her red-tipped fingernails glided the zipper of her robe past the enticing valley between her breasts, past the teasing glimpse of her navel, to stop at the point that intrigued him the most, making it undeniably clear that she was completely naked beneath the crimson robe.

She let it fall to the plush carpet and the tip of his tongue darted out to wet his suddenly dry lips. He took a shuddering breath as he fumbled with the buttons of his own shirt. Quickly disposed of his clothing, he joined her reclining form amid the plump down comforter and the numerous pillows that cushioned her long, slender body so enticingly.

Her skin was a warm toasty hue against the peach-colored satin sheets. Her dark eyes fluttered closed in keen pleasure as his fingertip lightly circled her breast, then cupped the burgeoning fullness in his palm. The pad

184

of his thumb was tantalizingly rough against the tip that hardened immediately beneath his mastery.

Deftly, he lifted her to her knees and his head dipped to reach his lips to the dusty-coral tip. Her head lolled back with the incredible sensual pleasure he could bestow with the mere flick of his tongue as he moved across the downy valley to the other one.

His hands moved to span her hips, cupping her behind as his lips raced down her rib cage to circle her navel in a maddeningly erotic maneuver. Her body tensed, inflamed with desire as his descent continued until he had captured the very essence of her wanting.

Relief and contentment washed through her, but the respite was only momentary as his tongue worked its magic, building the tension within her, fanning the flames into a raging need for completeness. Her hands gripped his biceps, her nails digging into the muscled flesh.

He needed no more encouragement than the soft moaning of his name from her lips. His mouth found her lips, stifling her cry of ecstasy when he joined her body with his. For several seconds, he didn't move, but shudders of satisfaction wracked through them both.

Alinda was the one that refused to let him hold back, refused to let him gather even a meager amount of composure. Her hips began to undulate slowly beneath him.

He tried pressing her into the mattress, but her writhing only increased his lack of control. "Ali, if you don't stop, I won't be able to prolong this much longer. You're driving me mad." He pulled away sharply and exhaled hard.

Alinda arched her body to meet his. Her legs tangled around his back, forcing him to stay within her. Her hands skated over him, her fingernails brushing the corded veins in his neck, foraging through his muscular chest and down his hard torso, grazing the top of his thighs, up his hips. The tender tips of her fingers bit into the hard contours of his back, urging him to satisfy them both.

With a defeated groan, he pinned her to the mattress with his hips, his arms stiff at either side of her shoulders as he began to move faster and faster, each stroke more powerful than the last. She held fast to his waist. Their hearts took flight, soaring to freedom together, on wings of a thousand tiny butterflies. An incandescent glow from within lit their way through the long flight of ecstasy and as they floated back to reality, free and easy.

He collapsed on top of her after the magical, mystical ride. His arms surrounded her waist and rolled to his back, taking her with him.

After his breathing slowed and he could think rationally once again, he smiled inwardly at the thought of how long it would take Alinda's curiosity to get the best of her. He predicted less than five minutes and he was right.

"I must know what happened. I'm dying of curiosity." She raised up on her elbows and ran a loving finger along his bruised jaw.

"Hasn't that curiosity gotten you into enough trouble?" The look he directed at her was stern and censorial. But he couldn't keep the mock-stern expression on his face. A smile broke out, the smile that only she could pull from the deepest part of his soul. At her look of impatience, he pressed a warm kiss to her forehead and without preamble, he explained everything.

"When I left the ranch, I fully intended to drive as far from here as possible, to never see you again. But after a few hours, I couldn't go on, not without you. I stopped at a pay phone and called my contact and he confirmed my suspicions. They had been using me as a decoy." He told her the conversation he had had with Baker and the plan that he agreed to follow.

"You could have been killed!"

"I could have, but I wasn't." Her breathing quickened and the fine lines across her brow deepened. He rushed on. "It's all over. Don't look so worried. Bianco and the two men that broke into the cabin are in jail and will be for a long time." Running his hands through his hair, he admitted, "It's been one hell of a long day. I could use another hug."

She went into his arms without hesitation. "Baker arranged for transportation to an island in the South Pacific. Will you go there with me, Ali?" He held his breath, suddenly wondering what he would do if she said no. Now that the truth was out would she lose interest in him? Would she decide his life was too complicated, too sorted, to build a future with him?

"What do you mean Baker arranged it for you? Aren't you free? Can't you resume your own name, use the identity you were born with?"

"Yes, but I want you away from here until the trial is over and the publicity dies down. I don't want to take any chances."

"Oh, I see," she said dejectedly, laying her head back down on his shoulder where he couldn't see the disappointment in her face. Was his only concern for her safety? He had offered her a brief trip to paradise, not a permanent relationship. It made sense. He hadn't had any freedom for four years. Why would he want to tie himself down just as it was handed back to him? Could she spend a few weeks with him and then survive giving him up?

"I don't think you understand, or at least I hope you

187

don't, since you have such a long face." He took her hands and kissed the backs of each one before looking directly into her dark eyes. "I want you to marry me, Ali. I know I don't have much to offer right now, but that will change as soon as the trial is over and I can lead a normal life again."

Her eyes lit up, then became troubled again. "You won't go back to work for the government, will you?" she asked fearfully.

"No. I'll have to come back to testify, but I won't work for them anymore." He hugged her to him so tightly she lost her breath.

Suddenly the crystalline blue of his eyes darkened and he turned gravely serious. "Every mile I drove away from you was agony. All I could think about was how your hair looked unbound and cascading across the pillow, those obsidian eyes of yours smoldering with passion, what it would be like to make love with you every day and night for the rest of my life." His whispers of love became throaty yearnings as he moved from her ear to her throat, stopping to flick his tongue at the hollow of its base. He felt her swallow anxiously. "You can't imagine the hell I went through thinking I'd never hold you again."

Seriously, her hand cupped his face. "Yes, I can." Tears of love shimmered in her dark eyes and he tenderly wiped the lone drop that slipped down her cheek.

"You just cannot know how wonderful this is. To lie beside you without fear or questions or mistrust. To ask you the things my heart has wanted to for weeks. It's like a dream come true."

Suddenly, mischievously, she said, "And you said you were all out of hopes and dreams and happily-ever-afters."

188

"Didn't I tell you? Recently, I stumbled on to enough of them to last me a lifetime." He stroked her back for several minutes, lazily nuzzling the sensitive swell of her breast in the early-morning quiet.

The birds were beginning to sing lightly in the aftermath of the storm that had blown over with hardly a drop of rain released from the heavy winter clouds. From the bed, he stared out the arched window, set high in the east wall. He tried to concentrate on the sunrise as it peeked above the horizon, tentatively streaking the sky in fuchsia and turquoise. But a deep impatient breath filled his lungs as he nervously broached the subject that would determine the course of the rest of his life.

"You haven't answered my question," he said peevishly. "Are you trying to let me down easy?" His composure suddenly left him. His hand shook slightly at her waist.

"Yes, I'll marry you and yes, I'll honeymoon with you in the South Pacific and yes, I'll live with you happily ever after." Her voice did not waver and neither did her eyes stray from his, even in the emotionally charged atmosphere. She was confident in her decision to spend her life with this fiercely intense yet gentle man.

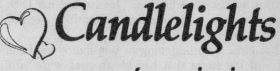